"There's som... ~~wanted to try.~~

"Do tell." Trent smiled. "What does a nice girl like you think about alone in the deep of night?"

And in her whiskey-induced honesty, Chloe told him. Every lurid, naughty detail of every lurid, naughty fantasy she'd ever had. By the time she was finished, his eyes blazed with desire and his body was obviously more than eager to play along.

"I don't think we can get to all of that tonight, Chloe, but we can definitely make a dent in your list." He rolled out of bed and fetched her discarded panty hose. With quick efficiency, he tied her wrists together and then to the headboard and knelt between her knees, his eyes burning with dark fire.

"Let's see just how far you're willing to go, my nice, normal little accountant."

Dear Reader,

This was one of those books that burst into life, hit the ground running and never looked back. It's always a special treat for me when a pair of characters take over the story and drag me along purely to act as their typist. Chloe and Trent sent me on a particularly wild ride, and I really had to type fast to keep up with them.

Chloe was a ton of fun. It was a challenge to write the sibling of a former heroine and to find a completely unique story for her even though Chloe and her sister came from essentially the same background. Trent continues my exploration of the limits of current science and what the near future may look like. I continue to be amazed at how close we are to having abilities like Trent and the other members of the Code X team.

And then, of course, there was the sizzling chemistry between Chloe and Trent to capture on the page without burning it to ashes. Throw in a bad guy or two, attempted murder and kidnapping, and we've got a recipe for a fun read.

So pour yourself your favorite beverage, order out so you don't have to cook supper, relax, put your feet up and dive into a flash of death, mayhem and true love!

Until next time, happy reading…

Cindy Dees

CINDY DEES

Flash of Death

HARLEQUIN®

entertain, enrich, inspire™

Recycling programs
for this product may
not exist in your area.

ISBN-13: 978-0-373-27796-4

FLASH OF DEATH

www.Harlequin.com

Printed in U.S.A.

Books by Cindy Dees

CINDY DEES

started flying airplanes while sitting in her dad's lap at the age of three and got a pilot's license before she got a driver's license. At age fifteen, she dropped out of high school and left the horse farm in Michigan, where she grew up, to attend the University of Michigan. After earning a degree in Russian and East European studies, she joined the U.S. Air Force and became the youngest female pilot in its history. She flew supersonic jets, VIP airlift and the C-5 Galaxy, the world's largest airplane. During her military career, she traveled to forty countries on five continents, was detained by the KGB and East German secret police, got shot at, flew in the first Gulf War and amassed a lifetime's worth of war stories.

Her hobbies include medieval reenacting, professional Middle Eastern dancing and Japanese gardening.

This RITA® Award-winning author's first book was published in 2002 and since then she has published more than twenty-five best-selling and award-winning novels. She loves to hear from readers and can be contacted at www.cindydees.com.

Kathy, you keep me sane even when I accept insane deadlines. Thanks for everything. You're the best!

Chapter 1

Chloe Jordan knew one thing: the combination of turning thirty and being one of the only single women at her little sister's wedding was thoroughly depressing—expensive-chocolate-and-cheap-wine-binge depressing. The hell of it was that she, as the maid of honor, emphasis on *maid, old* maid, had an ironclad obligation to be the life of the party. No matter how much she loved her little sis, this night officially sucked.

A chorus of spoons knocking on glasses startled her out of her momentary slip into melancholy. Shouts of laughter went up as the groom laid a smoking-hot kiss on the bride. *Sheesh. Somebody throw a bucket of ice water on those two.*

Chloe checked her bitterness. Sunny'd had a really crappy run of luck and deserved all the happiness she could get. The lucky groom, Aiden, obviously loved Sunny fiercely. Next up on her personal hit parade of depressing events was bound to be playing indulgent auntie to their perfect children. Yippee.

The band resumed playing too loudly to talk over, and thankfully a mob of guests piled out of their seats, relieving her of any duty to go out onto a painfully empty dance floor and "get things started."

It didn't help her mood that she'd had a little too much champagne and was starting to feel a little weepy. Sunny was so beautiful and radiant, and she was so proud of her little sis. Chloe noticed from her seat jammed in the corner that it had started raining outside.

One of the groomsmen got the bright idea to light up a cigar, and furthermore, to pass out cigars to all the other groomsmen. A cloud of noxious blue smoke enveloped her. Her stomach roiled ominously.

Enough was enough. She took her queasy stomach and crazy mood swings and fled the reception in search of fresh air. She burst out of the private club that was one of Denver's most exclusive addresses and inhaled deeply. But even the rain wouldn't give her a break and the skies opened up without warning. Her hotel was right across the street and she ran for it, racing down the club's wide steps. Streetlights glittered off the wet pavement as she dashed between cars.

She never saw it coming.

A big, dark SUV accelerated toward her out of nowhere, its engine growling hungrily as it shot forward. Its headlights were blinding and she stared into them in shock.

The impact was incredible, knocking her completely off her feet and sending her flying through space splayed out on her back. Something powerful wrapped around her torso, yanking her in a midair one-eighty so she landed on her stomach. She slammed into something…

…and didn't die horribly. Whatever she'd smashed into

had definitely been hard but not nearly as unyielding as concrete. Her breath was knocked clean out of her, though, and she gasped frantically to no avail. Disoriented, she stared down at the man lying beneath her. Had she been thrown into him and knocked him down?

An engine revved and tires squealed behind her. She looked up in time to see a black, shiny, wet SUV disappear around a corner at a high speed.

She'd nearly died. And the man lying so still beneath her had probably saved her life by breaking her fall. Had she *killed* him? All of a sudden, she was able to breathe again. She sucked in a sobbing breath and rolled off of the man.

"Are you okay?" she asked urgently.

His eyes blinked open, and silver eyes stared up at her, laser-intense. Eyes she recognized. Ohmigosh. He was one of Aiden's groomsmen. Trenton something. Hollings. That was it. She'd heard some of the other guys call him Trent.

"I'll live," he rasped. "You?"

"I'm fine. You broke my fall. I'm so sorry—"

He cut her off. "No need to apologize. Who was in that car?"

"I don't know. I didn't see anything, and then those headlights were coming at me. I guess the SUV hit me and sent me flying into you."

"Actually," he murmured, sitting up carefully, his dark hair tousled and sexy, "I'm the only thing that hit you. I knocked you out of the car's way at the last second. Had that SUV hit you, something that heavy moving that fast would have killed you instantly."

She stared, stunned anew. He really *had* saved her life. For a man who'd just been knocked flat by a human-sized flying object, he popped to his feet with a speed and grace that shocked her. A hand materialized in front of her eyes.

It was big and tanned and calloused in stark contrast to the pristinely starched white cuff and onyx cufflink above it.

She took his hand and floated to her feet.

"Are you sure you're all right?" he asked, his voice deep. Rough with concern.

She looked down at her red silk gown ruefully. The side seam had torn from the hem almost all the way to her hip. Her slender leg was entirely exposed. "I'm fine. But I can't say the same for my dress."

He looked down critically. "I like it better like this. A woman with legs like yours should show them off."

Her startled gaze lifted to his, and he smiled at her. But not just any smile, rather a sizzling hot one that promised a long night of steamy seduction if she was interested. She about fell off her three-inch stilettos in shock. Trenton Hollings was flirting with her? The hottest groomsman out of a whole batch of ridiculously hot men? No way.

He offered her his forearm, and she looped her hand around it in minor shock. The hard muscles beneath the soft Italian wool contracted sharply. "Ready to try crossing the street again?" he murmured.

"I swear, I looked both ways. I never saw that car coming. One second the street was clear, and the next, there it was, running me down."

Trent nodded, frowning. "I believe you." His frown deepened as they stepped gingerly back out into the wide boulevard. They managed to cross to the other side of the street without incident, although her escort did pause as they reached the far curb to take a long look back over his shoulder at the scene of her near miss.

"What's on your mind?" she asked cautiously.

Her words seemed to jolt him out of his reverie and he gave himself a little shake. "Getting you up to your room in one piece and cleaned up is on my mind."

She looked down at herself in alarm. Just how bad did she look? As if it mattered. She was darned lucky just to be alive, for goodness' sake. They stepped into a hotel elevator, and in the small, enclosed space, her tall escort dwarfed her. She was not short herself at five foot seven, plus three inches of heels, but he still had several inches on her. He was muscular without being thick. His shoulders filled out his tuxedo nicely, and well-defined biceps flexed within his sleeves. No wonder the impact of him slamming into her had knocked her halfway across the street.

"Do you save women from being run down a lot?" she asked to fill the silence.

His mouth twitched in humor. "Not often."

"What do you do when you're not doing that?"

He shrugged. "I'm a bum."

She blinked, startled. "You clean up pretty well for a bum."

A full-fledged grin flashed her way, all but knocking her off her feet again. Nobody got teeth that perfect and white without expensive orthodontic work. And that tuxedo was no rental monkey suit. It was cashmere with Italian lines exquisitely tailored to his athletic physique. Not to mention Sunny'd told her how wealthy and successful all of Aiden's groomsmen were, not so subtly hinting that Chloe should pick one and go for the gusto. The guys had all gone to college together, apparently. Frat brothers, in fact. And most of them worked with billionaire Jeff Winston at Winston Enterprises. Bum. Right.

"Tell me another lie," she murmured.

"You're ugly and not the slightest bit sexy."

Her gaze snapped to his. "Excuse me?"

"You asked for a lie."

Before she could think up a snappy comeback the elevator door opened and he reached an arm out to hold it open. His free hand came to rest lightly in the middle of her back as he shepherded her out. She felt surrounded by him, and it was the strangest sensation. Maybe it was because she was with men so rarely, or maybe it was because he was so freaking hot, but either way, her breath shortened disconcertingly.

As she exited the elevator, her heel caught in the door's track and stuck momentarily, pitching her off balance. Instantly, Trent's strong hand was on her elbow, steadying her. "I'm such a klutz," she mumbled.

"Good thing for you I'm not," he replied wryly.

She started down the hallway toward the snazzy suite Aiden had insisted on paying for. Chloe wasn't penniless anymore, but she surely wouldn't have wasted so much money on an extravagant hotel room that, outside of sleeping and showering, she'd spent about five minutes awake in each day.

She glanced sidelong at Trent. "Are you one of those athletic people who always manage to land on their feet and make the rest of us mere mortals look silly?"

He shrugged modestly.

She sighed. "That's what I thought." As she fumbled with her room's key card, he lifted it from her shaking fingers. Wow. That near miss with the SUV must have rattled her worse than she'd realized.

"Let me get that." He reached past her to open the door and then did a strange thing. He put a restraining hand on her arm. "Wait here."

She frowned as he disappeared into the dark suite. He was back in a minute, flipping on light switches as he came. What was that all about?

"What are you standing out here for?" he asked.

"You told me to—" She broke off as she caught the

glint of humor in his silver eyes. Dry sense of humor this guy had.

She followed him into the suite.

"When did you get into town?" he asked as he moved over to the picture windows and inexplicably pulled the blinds closed on a magnificent view of Denver's night lights glittering in the rain.

"Three days ago."

His brows flickered. "And you haven't had time to unpack?"

She glanced around the suite, startled. "I am unpacked. Clothes in the closet, toothbrush in the bathroom."

"Jeez. The room doesn't even look occupied. Are you always this…neat?"

"Well, yes." There was nothing wrong with order. It made life infinitely easier. She could always lay hands on exactly what she wanted when she wanted it.

"And what do you do for a living, Chloe?"

She winced at his question. She'd give anything to do something exotic and sexy that would impress this man. But she was who she was. She sighed and answered reluctantly, "I'm a forensic accountant."

"What does that mean? You do dead people's taxes?"

She smiled. "No. It means I take apart companies' books and find the discrepancies they may or may not be trying to hide."

"You're some sort of auditor, then?"

"Not exactly. Forensic accountants are used mostly in criminal investigations to find the money trail."

"Who do you work for?" Trent asked.

"I'm a freelance consultant at the moment."

"Sounds…interesting."

She laughed. "About as interesting as watching grass

grow, right? Actually, I find the work fascinating. But I don't expect other people to get it."

He wandered around the suite examining every detail, and although she enjoyed the view of him from so many angles, she was eventually prompted to ask, "Are you always so restless?"

"Hmm, what? Oh. Yes."

"And what do you do for a living?"

"Nothing."

She frowned. "How do you support yourself, then?"

He stopped roaming and turned to face her in surprise. "You mean you can't smell the trust fund at a hundred yards? I thought all women could do that."

"Sorry. Not me." Trust fund, huh? Big enough that he didn't have to work at all? Must be nice.

He resumed roaming, poking around behind the bar. "Aha!" he crowed. He turned around with a bottle of whiskey in hand. She recognized the label vaguely as an expensive single-malt variety.

"So, how do you fill your time if you don't work?" she asked curiously. She'd put in sixty- and eighty-hour weeks for so long, juggling bookkeeping jobs and school while she got her accounting degree and master's in forensic accounting she couldn't imagine doing anything else.

He set two shot glasses side by side on the wet bar and poured generous shots of amber liquid into each. He looked up at her and grinned. "I play for a living."

Play? She couldn't ever remember a time when she'd done that. Maybe when her folks were still alive. But even then, her hippie parents had been such flakes about money that she'd ended up taking over the family finances before she'd turned ten. She'd always been more of an adult than anyone else in the Jordan clan. And when her parents died in a boating accident halfway around the world from her and Sunny, orphaning them at ages thirteen and ten respectively, she'd grown up for real. Fast.

Trent thrust a shot glass at her and, startled out of her grim thoughts, she took it.

"Drink up. You need it."

She frowned down at the whiskey.

"You had a bad shock and your nerves are fried. Think of it as medicine," he coaxed.

Mentally holding her nose, she lifted the shot glass and tossed down the shot of whiskey in a single gulp. Fire exploded in her throat and roared down into her belly. She coughed and swore as tears streamed down her face. Trent, the cad, laughed as she mopped at her eyes.

He neatly downed his own shot and went back to the bar for refills. When he came back with another shot glass for her, she waved it off.

"Second time, it goes down as smooth as silk. I promise."

She snorted. "That's because every nerve in my digestive track is incinerated at the moment."

He smiled winningly. "Exactly."

"I shouldn't. I've already had too much champagne—" she started.

He cut her off gently. "Don't overthink it. Just trust me. You need this."

She *did* have a tendency to talk herself out of everything fun in life. And she was safely in her hotel room with a man her sister swore was a great guy. That pleasant, warm feeling spreading outward from her belly button really was very nice, too. She took the second shot and slammed it back before she could change her mind.

This time it made her feel light-headed. A little silly, even. Just what the doctor ordered.

"Another?" Trent asked.

"Are you trying to get me drunk, sir?"

He grinned unrepentantly. "I am."

"Why?" she blurted. Whoops. She hadn't meant to say that out loud, but it just slipped out all by itself.

He answered, "You've looked uptight all day long."

"I am not uptight!"

"Honey, if you were wound too much tighter, you'd snap in two."

Okay, she was starting to feel a little dizzy. But nice dizzy. Like she wanted to throw her arms out and dance to the sensation.

"Why don't we get you out of those shoes?" Trent murmured, guiding her over to the edge of her bed and sitting her down on it. He knelt at her feet, sliding his big hand down the back of her calf with sensual leisure. "I never have been able to understand why women wear these things. They look blasted uncomfortable."

He tossed one red shoe over his shoulder and she giggled as she wiggled her toes. "But heels make our legs look so nice," she explained earnestly.

"You don't need any help to make your legs look great," he announced as the other red stiletto went flying.

She stood up and hiked up her torn skirt enough to reach under it. It occurred to her in a distant corner of her mind that she would never, under normal circumstances, do something as intimate as take off her hose in front of a man like this. She stated, "Now if you want to know what's really uncomfortable and stupid in women's fashion, it's panty hose."

She started to peel hers down, but then warm, strong hands were there, pushing her fingers aside.

"Let me get those for you." His hands were a warm slide down her thighs, leaving a trail of wanton destruction in their wake. As her legs positively wobbled, she grabbed his shoulders to steady herself. She lifted first one foot and then the other so he could remove her hose.

"I say we outlaw panty hose," he declared as hers went flying over his shoulder.

She laughed gaily. "I second the motion."

"Turn around," he instructed.

She did so and was startled to feel her gown's long zipper sliding down. Cool air caressed her back. Warm hands kneaded her shoulders and she let her head fall forward with a groan of pleasure. His clever fingers went right to the massive knot that perennially twisted at the base of her neck.

"Are you always this tense?" he asked. His voice was smooth and deep and warmed her from the outside the same way the whiskey warmed her from the inside.

"Pretty much," she answered honestly.

"Do you need me to do something about it?"

He already was. The knot was unraveling beneath his fingers like magic. And then his clever plan dawned on her. She craned her head around to look at him over her shoulder. "Are you seducing me?"

"Would you like me to?"

"Well, duh. You're a complete hunk. But me? What would a guy like you see in a girl like me?"

He laughed softly. "Have you looked at yourself in a mirror? You're a knockout. Not too many women can pull off sophisticated and pure-as-the-driven-snow in the same look." He ticked off her additional attributes with his fingers against the side of her neck. "You make me laugh. And you're smart or you wouldn't be a forensic accountant. And you have a kind heart or you wouldn't have suffered through your sister's wedding with a smile on your face all day."

"I didn't suffer—"

"Sure you did. Anyone who really looked at you could see it in your eyes. The way I hear it, you practically raised her. She's your only family and she's starting a new life with someone else. No matter how much you love her, that has to hurt. Has to make you feel all alone in the world."

What a perceptive man to have noticed. And he must have a pretty kind heart himself to be here comforting her like this. "You're right, of course," she murmured. As the truth of his words sank in, a knife of grief and loss stabbed at her heart. She'd faced terrible loss in her life, agonizing loneliness. But this was right up there. *Oh, Sunny. I'm gonna miss you so much.* Tears sprang to her eyes.

She started to turn around to face Trent, but his big hands forestalled her. And then something warm and resilient moved against her neck where it joined her shoulder.

"You're not alone, tonight," he murmured against her skin.

Desperate need for that to be true had her leaning back toward him, her whole being reaching out toward the solace he offered. Just once in her life, she would love for someone to be strong for her, to take care of her. His hands moved slowly across her stomach, easing her back against him even more closely as if he was telling her to lean on him. But if his hands were there, what was that touching her neck?

His mouth! As realization dawned, a host of delicious sensations ripped through her, radiating outward from where his lips moved across her skin. Languor and lust rolled through her, making a beeline for her knees and threatening to collapse them. Whiskey, thy name is temptation.

Was she seriously going to do this? Trent Hollings? The bachelor every female at the wedding had been throwing herself at? Of course, he'd been the one to throw himself at her. Literally.

"Tell me again not to overthink this," she muttered.

He turned her around then, his hands unerringly finding every hairpin and tossing them aside. He plunged both hands into her thick, blond hair and pulled the French twist down around her shoulders in lush waves. Her hair was her secret pride, and she was glad he could see it like this. She never wore it down in her daily life. In her career field, she needed people to take her seriously and not treat her like some kind of sex kitten. But tonight, she was okay with that. If Trent Hollings thought she was hot, she was darned well not about to talk him out of it.

"Mmm. Better," he murmured. "I've been itching to do that all day."

"Really?"

He took her face in his big hands and tilted it up to his. "Really."

She tensed as his head lowered toward hers. He paused, his mouth inches from hers, and breathed, "Don't overthink this."

Right. Live in the moment. Go for it. *Carpe diem.* His lips touched hers and the platitudes fled in the face of this stunningly sexy man kissing her. His mouth was warm and smooth and confident, and in about ten seconds, he'd blasted past all her experience in kissing. His lips parted hers and his tongue tested her teeth. She gasped at the invasion and he took immediate advantage of it to taste her more deeply.

His arms tightened around her, lifting her against his big, warm body. A hand slid up her back to her head, cradling it in a large palm and drawing her even further into the kiss. And then he was kissing her with his whole body. Whether that was him moving against her or her moving against him she couldn't tell and didn't care. Her dress gaped open in the back and his hand burned her bare flesh as it dipped inside the gown. She was shocked when his hand slid down to cup her derriere and… Oh, God, she'd forgotten she was wearing that silly thong Sunny'd talked her into. Something about panty lines ruining the lie of the gown.

He made a sound of surprised approval.

"What?" she blurted.

"I didn't peg you for a naughty-lingerie kind of girl."

Painfully aware of the drawer full of cotton granny panties across the room, she didn't disabuse him of the notion. For the first time all day, she was grateful for the tiny scrap of spandex and lace nestled a little too intimately in her nether regions. Trent's finger traced the thin line of the thong downward and she groaned in pleasure and embarrassment.

"You're overthinking," he warned laughingly. "Let go and enjoy yourself."

Her knees did buckle then. He caught her up against him with ease and kissed her with gusto until her knees would bear her weight again. "Ahh, you're going to be a joy to seduce. So artless. So natural. Such a nice young lady."

"Is that bad?" she asked, frowning up at two of him swimming in her gaze. She did believe she was officially buzzed.

"Not at all." His fingers slipped under the shoulders of the lined gown with its built-in shelf bra. Which meant she wasn't wearing a blessed thing under the gown. Except that sexy little black thong, of course. He hooked the red silk and slipped it off her shoulders, kissing her skin as it was revealed. The gown whispered down her body to the floor in a bloodred puddle and she shivered. Whether it was the cool air on her skin or Trent's hot mouth on her skin that caused it, she couldn't say.

"You're magnificent, Chloe. How is it some man hasn't snatched you up and made you his?"

She blinked up at Trent as he straightened and shrugged off his tuxedo jacket. Nope, no padding in them there shoulders. His starched, white shirt clung to a physique that could make a girl weep with appreciation. Realizing belatedly that she was all but drooling at him, she answered, enunciating carefully so she wouldn't slur her words, "I'm too boring. And neat. Men hate neat."

Trent laughed as he stripped off his cummerbund and tossed it aside. "That's not how I hear it. Most men love a woman who'll pick up after them. When I settle down, I'll hire a butler to do the job. It'll save on resentment from the ladies in my life."

Ladies. Plural. Of course a man like him had scads of women chasing after him. "I'm just one more in a long string of conquests, aren't I?" she accused. Who knew whiskey brought out such a brutally honest streak in her?

He laughed lightly. "Never. You're one of a kind, Chloe Jordan."

At least he knew her full name. The way she heard it, that was an exception for most pick-up artists. For surely, this man was a master of the art. And yet, she couldn't bring herself to care as his hands slid over her ribs and cupped her breasts, lifting them and testing their weight. She wasn't all that stacked, although she'd always privately thought her breasts were rather nicely shaped. Trent seemed to think so, too, as his mouth captured one pert, rosy peak and sucked gently. Lightning bolts started at his mouth and spread outward through her body.

"Oh, my," she sighed. "That's lovely."

A strong arm swept behind her knees and she was

tipped on her side all of a sudden as he picked her up and laid her on the bed. The down comforter gave beneath her weight, and the room spun lightly around her. And then Trent was there, stretched out beside her, propped up on one elbow, yanking the knot out of his bow tie with his free hand. Shirt studs went flying as he jerked his shirt free of his trousers and all but tore it off.

She reached up to help push the shirt off his shoulders and gaped as acres of tanned chest appeared before her eyes. "Yowza," she breathed.

He laughed heartily and she glared up at him. "Are you laughing at me?" she demanded.

"Yes, I am. It has been a while since I've gotten that sort of reaction out of a woman from taking off my shirt."

"Do you only date blind women?" she retorted.

He leaned close to kiss her lightly before answering, "No. Jaded ones. Like I said, you're one of a kind."

"Hey. I didn't fall off the pumpkin truck yesterday, you know. I live in San Francisco and work at a very up-scale address. Of course, I'm going to take that company down, but—"

He stopped her rambling with his mouth against hers. She wasn't sure how he got his trousers off or how the covers got thrown back, but in a moment, she was lying on her back on Egyptian cotton sheets with a thread count so high they felt like velvet against her skin, and Trent was stretched out in all his naked, unconcerned glory beside her.

"Please tell me you're a little bit drunk, too," she muttered.

He grinned, flashing that million-dollar smile at her again. "I'm drunk on you, baby."

She rolled her eyes and he laughed back at her. He really was incorrigible. But then the smile faded from his eyes, leaving them a dark, smoky gray that pierced through her whiskey-induced fog like high-beam headlights. All of a sudden, heat radiated from him. A promise of sex so steamy it would burn away all the fog and bring the night down around them.

Her breath caught on a gasp as, without breaking his gaze into her eyes, his hand traveled down the valley between her breasts, across the flat plane of her belly, and hooked inside the thong that was her only remaining defense. His fingers slid across soft flesh that was so sensitive she thought she was going to come apart this very second.

And then his fingers dipped lower, sliding across strangely swollen flesh that raged with lust in response to his touch. "Whoa!" she exclaimed.

He froze against her. "What's wrong?"

"Nothing's wrong!"

"Then why did you yell for me to stop?" he asked cautiously.

It took her whiskey-fuzzed brain a moment to sort that one out. Then she blurted, "Oh. I get it. No. I was reacting to how great that felt. You know. As in, whoa, that's awesome, dude."

He burst out laughing. "So you don't want me to stop?"

"No!"

"You have no idea how glad I am to hear that," he murmured. For a second time, the humor fled from his gaze, leaving behind a raw, sexual hunger in his eyes that completely undid her. Men never looked at her like that. And certainly not men like him.

He whisked the thong off her and it joined her other clothes somewhere across the room. And then he did that surrounding her thing again, all muscle and heat and impatient man. The room spun more wildly now. Where the whiskey stopped and the intoxication of this man making love to her took over, she couldn't rightly say. It was a heady cocktail, though.

His muscular thigh nudged hers apart and she tensed. He stared down at her as if waiting for her to say something.

"I'm overthinking again, aren't I?" she mumbled.

"Relax. Enjoy. Let go."

His voice was so darned seductive. It was so easy to sink into the pleasure of the moment, to lose herself in the whirling lights and giddy lust dancing around her and in her.

His other thigh joined the first one, and he levered her legs wide apart. This time she arched toward him with a soft cry of need. If she was going to do this, then by golly, she was really going to go for it. She flung caution to the wind and launched herself toward him. He caught her up against his shockingly hard body and kissed her deeply. And then he took her. There wasn't another word for it. He invaded boldly, filling her to the point of delicious discomfort, and then he made her his. Fast then slow, gently and then with driving force, he made love to her.

When she would have closed her eyes, embarrassed over how wantonly she was throwing herself at him, he wouldn't stand for it and made her open her eyes to look at him. When she would have shrunk away from the hoarse cries of pleasure torn from her own throat, he kissed her until she gave those cries to him. And when he drove her to release a second and even a third time, he ripped away any last vestiges of inhibition she might have clung to, with the sheer excess of pleasure he gave her.

Her entire being was raw and exposed to him. He played her body and soul like the master artist he was before he finally joined her in one last, shattering climax. It tore his name from her throat on a primal note she'd never sung before. It was, in a word, magnificent. And better yet, she wasn't alone.

He collapsed beside her on the now-damp sheets, breathing heavily. She rolled over and pushed up on his chest to stare down at him, and that was when the full broadside of the whiskey hit her. Dizzy and reckless, she retained just enough reason to know this was a once-in-a-lifetime opportunity for a girl like her. One not to be missed.

"If I let you rest a little, do you think we could do that again?" she asked.

A broad grin spread across his face.

She added hastily, "Well, not that exactly. There's something else I've always wanted to try…"

"Do tell. What does a nice girl like you think about alone in the deep of night?"

And in her whiskey-induced honesty, she told him. Every lurid, naughty detail of every lurid, naughty fantasy she'd ever had. By the time she was finished, his eyes blazed with desire and his body was obviously more than eager to play along.

"I don't think we can get to all of that tonight, Chloe, but we can definitely make a dent in your list." He rolled out of bed and fetched her discarded panty hose. With quick efficiency, he tied her wrists together and then to the headboard and knelt between her knees, his eyes burning with dark fire.

"Let's see just how far you're willing to go, my nice, normal little accountant."

Chapter 2

Trent slipped out of the hotel's delivery entrance in the last dark before dawn. He couldn't sleep anyway, and there was no sense humiliating Chloe by strolling out through the hotel lobby in his rumpled tuxedo for all the staff to see.

Normally, he would've spent the night in her bed and enjoyed a morning-after brunch with her, but he had a hunch that, after last night, she'd just as soon wake up alone. For one thing, she was going to have a hell of a hangover. And, if she was telling the truth and had never done any of the things they'd done together last night, he'd lay odds she was going to suffer a rather large dose of morning-after embarrassment. He hadn't been kidding when he called her a nice girl.

Who'd have guessed such a prim-and-proper lady would be such a wildcat after a few shots of whiskey? She'd pushed even a few of his sexual boundaries last night, and that was saying something. He'd spent most of his post-pubescent life enjoying the favors of beautiful women. But he'd never met one quite like Chloe Jordan, all sweet and virginal in public, and jaw-droppingly *not* virginal in private.

He crossed the street, stopping at the spot where the SUV had nearly run her down last night. As he'd thought. Not a skid mark in sight. That vehicle had *accelerated* toward her. Now why would anyone be out to hurt an uptight accountant who lived and worked half a continent away?

And more importantly, who would want to kill her?

Frowning, he returned to his own suite in the men's club where the wedding had been held. His family owned the apartment, and he used it when he was in town. As its dark wood, leather and Ralph Lauren décor surrounded him, he breathed in the easy, old-world elegance with guilty pleasure. Most of the time he shunned the trappings of his family's wealth. He was much more likely to be found in a shack on a beach, waxing a surfboard than lounging in high-end men's clubs. And frankly, he was more at ease in the shack. People were more real there. Had a better sense of what really mattered in life.

Being diagnosed with his illness in his second year of college had put everything in perspective for him. Life was too short to waste doing things or being around people who made him crazy.

But he had to admit, this condo's luxury was nice once in a while.

He took a six-jet steam shower to work out the worst of the kinks from last night's athletics with Chloe, and shaved and dressed quickly. Then he sat down at the walnut desk in the corner and made a phone call to Winston Ops.

It was the headquarters of a private, corporate intelligence network for all of the many Winston Enterprises companies around the world. The duty controller, a computer genius named Novak from somewhere in eastern Europe, took his call.

"Trent Hollings, here. I need you to run a quick background check for me on Chloe Jordan."

"Sunny's sister?" Novak asked, surprised.

"I think someone tried to kill her last night."

"Are you serious?" Novak exclaimed.

"As a heart attack."

The duty controller instantly shifted into all-business mode. "Got it. So, we're looking for enemies in her life." Trent heard clacking keys in the background as Novak typed furiously. "How was the wedding?"

"Great party," Trent answered. "Can't remember the last time I saw Aiden so happy. He's a lucky man."

"Maybe you should find yourself a nice girl and settle down, too."

He laughed. "Not me. I'll never slow down enough for any girl to catch me."

"When you least expect it, one's gonna come along and trip you all up, buddy."

Visions of a blonde accountant blowing his mind in bed flashed through his head. "Nah," Trent replied. "Not me. It's not like I can give any girl a life evenly faintly resembling normal." Hell, he couldn't even promise to give a girl children. With his inherited disorder, careful genetic counseling would be necessary to ensure that his condition—spinal muscular atrophy—wasn't passed on to his offspring.

"Okay, Trent. I've got a preliminary report on our girl. She's a certified public accountant. Just finished a master's degree in forensic accounting. Company called Paradeo filed a W-2 on her about six months ago. But they're an investment firm, not forensic accountants."

She'd said she was freelancing. And there'd been that reference to taking a company down. Must be investigating her employer for someone else. "Where's this Paradeo company headquartered?"

"San Francisco. No satellite offices. Anything else you need to know right away, Trent?"

"Do you see anything at a glance that could explain someone trying to run her down in a large SUV?"

"Other than some rich, pissed-off CEO she might have put in jail? Nope. You don't suppose it has anything to with Code X, do you?" Novak asked.

The controller's question made Trent's blood run cold. That was the one place he'd been mentally avoiding going this morning. He'd known it would give him exactly the headache he felt coming on. "I don't know. Keep digging and let's see what you come up with before we go there."

"Roger. I'm on it."

Trent paced the spacious room restlessly. He never had been able to sit still even before he'd accepted the experimental stem cell therapies that were both his miracle cure and the heart of the Code X project. Toss in a liberal dose of stress and worry now, and he could forget sitting down, let alone being still. He changed out of the clothes he'd donned only minutes before and into running gear. It was early enough that he should be able to stretch his legs a little without anyone seeing him.

He jogged down the stairs, too jumpy to wait for the elevator, and restrained himself until he'd cleared the lobby of the club. But when he hit the sidewalk, he couldn't contain the bursting energy any longer. He exploded into motion, sprinting down the street with strides that grew longer and faster with every step. In moments he was flying along at twenty-five miles per hour, the wind ripping through his hair and making his eyes water. God, it felt good.

Every time he ran like this, he remembered the early onset of his disease, the progressive muscle weakness, the loss of tendon strength, the continuous respiratory infections, the pain. And the fear. Not knowing what had been wrong with him was the worst of all as his body had literally wasted away before his eyes. It had taken over a year to get the diagnosis. SMA usually showed up in infants and small children, and it threw the doctors off when his case waited until adulthood to present itself.

A delivery truck backed out of an alley in front of him and he dodged around it with a lightning-fast move a professional football player would have envied.

He accelerated again, reveling in the flow of muscles and sinew and blood working in extraordinary harmony, his quick twitch muscles reacting completely off the charts for a normal human. But then, he wasn't normal at all. Not anymore. Not since Jeff Winston had called and suggested that there might be a radical cure for Trent's disease. It was highly experimental and had side effects, of course. He'd grabbed on to the lifeline his old friend had thrown him and never looked back. He was entirely and for the rest of his life a creature of Code X.

He ran for nearly an hour, slowing only when people began to emerge onto the streets and he risked someone seeing him race along at world-class sprinter speed for block after block.

He'd turned around to head back to the club when the cell phone in the breast pocket of his skin-tight running shirt vibrated. He slowed to a walk to take the call. It was his boss and friend, Jeff Winston.

"Hey, Jeff. What's up?"

"Couldn't you at least sound out of breath after tearing around like you do?" Jeff groused.

Thankfully, along with his quick twitch muscles had

come extraordinarily quick oxygen uptake. "Sorry, bro. I'll try to huff and puff a little. What can I do for you? It's early for you to be up, isn't it?"

"I need you here at the club ASAP. Take a cab."

"I can get there about as fast if I run."

"I don't need you drawing any attention to yourself just now," Jeff answered in clipped tones.

"What's going on?" Trent was alarmed. It was completely unlike Jeff to be this terse.

"When you get back."

Trent spotted a taxi stand and jogged to it at normal human speed, chafing at the slowness of the pace. He jumped into the first cab in line and gave the club's address. Had Novak uncovered something else about Chloe? Something that would explain her attempted murder? What on earth could it be?

The first thing Chloe became aware of was that her brain felt twice its normal size inside a skull that hadn't expanded one bit. Every beat of her heart sent throbbing pain through her head. As she swam slowly toward consciousness, she registered lying on her stomach among wildly tangled sheets and blankets, which was strange. Usually she was a quiet, neat sleeper who didn't disturb her bed much. And the rest of it registered. She was *naked*.

That startled her the rest of the way to full consciousness. She *never* slept in the buff. What if there was a fire and she had to race outside to safety? She rolled over onto her back and groaned as her entire body protested, sore. God, she felt like she'd been run over by a truck. Vague memory of that exact thing nearly happening tickled the edges of her fuzzy brain.

Memory of Trent came back to her. He'd been such a smooth operator, and she'd been so blessed eager to have him seduce her. Where was he now? Peeling one eyelid open, she groaned as sunlight creeping insidiously past the curtains pierced her skull like a sword. Agonizing pain exploded behind both eyes. No sign of Trent. He and his sexy tuxedo and bedroom eyes were gone. It was as if he'd never been here and knocked her world completely off its foundation.

The old hurt stabbed at her heart. Everybody always left her. Every time she took a chance on caring about some-one, she ended up all alone. Her parents. Her foster fami-lies. Even Sunny. They all abandoned her sooner or later. An urge to cry nearly overcame her. Was it too much just to want a normal life? To find a nice man, settle down in a modest home, have a few kids and a dog, and be happy?

By way of an answer, her stomach gave a mighty, and threatening, heave. Moaning in pain, she forced herself upright and ran for the toilet. After duly worshipping at the throne of the porcelain god and emptying what little remained in her stomach from last night's binge, she felt a few inches further away from death. But that wasn't saying much. A shower sounded good, but the idea of listening to the pounding of water sent her back to bed showerless.

She couldn't remember the last time she'd had a hang-over, and she'd never had one that even began to com-pare to this. Prepared to sleep for another, oh, decade, she crawled back into bed and threw an arm across her eyes.

A jangling noise that nearly split her skull in two made her swear and dive for her cell phone on the nightstand. "'Lo," she grumbled.

"Hey, sis! I missed you leaving the party last night."

Oh, God. Did Sunny have to sound so darned perky this morning? "Sorry. I drank a little too much champagne, and then some guys lit up cigars. The smoke made me nauseous, so I snuck out early."

"Rats. I was hoping some hot guy picked you up and took you back to his place."

Visions of the hot guy who'd knocked her off her feet, and then brought her back to her room and knocked her world completely out of orbit flashed into her mind.

Oh. My. God. Had she really asked him to… Had they really… She would never be able to look anyone from this wedding in the eye again… And she could never, ever, face *him* again… Mortification almost sent her back to the toilet a second time.

"Chloe? Are you still there?"

Her brain engaged belatedly. "Uhh, yeah. I'm here. Why are you calling me, anyway? Aren't you supposed to be on your honeymoon?"

"Aiden and I are at the airport. He won't tell me where we're going, but Jeff loaned us the Winston jet to get there. I just wanted to say goodbye. Aiden says I won't have phone service where we're headed."

"Wow. Sounds private and sexy. Have fun, eh?"

"It's my honeymoon and my hubby's a hottie. How can I not have fun?" Sunny retorted, laughing.

The cheerful sound nearly made Chloe's eyeballs fall right out of her head. She pressed a hand to them to hold them in. "Love you, baby sis."

"Love you, big sis."

Chloe groaned as she disconnected the call and turned her cell phone completely off. She prayed to sleep off the mother of all hangovers before she had to go back to San Francisco tomorrow. And then she prayed fervently that Trent Hollings would leave town today and go somewhere far, far away. Forever. There was no way she could ever look him in the eye after what they—what *she*—had done last night.

She took a solemn vow then and there never to touch

alcohol again as long as she lived. The idea of losing all her inhibitions like that again made her positively ill. Who'd have guessed a few shots of whiskey would turn her into such a slut?

Groaning in pain and embarrassment, she pulled the sheet up over her head and prayed for death. Or at least a long, long unconsciousness.

Trent burst into the conference room Jeff Winston had appropriated from the gentlemen's club to do business in while he was here for the wedding. Several of the other Code X operatives were there, complete with their own genetically engineered mutations, and they all looked worried.

"What the hell's going on?" he demanded without preamble.

Jeff answered, "Novak scared up some video from a traffic camera and ran the license plates of the SUV that tried to run down Chloe Jordan last night."

"And?"

"And it belongs to a corporation that doesn't exist."

Trent frowned. "Come again?"

"It's registered to a dummy company. Address is a P.O. box that doesn't exist, phone number is a fake and no company by that name is currently doing business in the United States. It's a cover for someone."

"Like who?" he asked his boss.

Jeff shrugged. "No idea. But it does lead me to believe it was no accident last night. Someone was out to hurt Chloe."

Trent replied grimly, "Wrong. Whoever gunned that SUV at her was out to *kill* her."

And that meant Code X had a problem. Chloe's sister had just married one of Code X's charter members—a guy who could hold his breath under water for over twelve minutes. And Chloe had spent the past two days in the company of the lot of them at various prewedding functions. How could her attempted murder *not* be aimed at the Code X team?

Trent suggested hopefully, "She said she's a forensic accountant. Maybe it was just a bit of revenge by an enemy she's made in her job."

"Possible," Jeff replied slowly. "If that's the case, we'll need a complete list of companies she has investigated." Trent watched as his boss pulled out his cell phone and dialed Chloe's cell phone number. As Jeff's frown deepened and he didn't speak into the device, Trent's apprehension grew.

Jeff put the phone down. "Her cell's turned off."

Trent winced. "She probably turned it off so schmucks like us wouldn't disturb her." She was *probably* sleeping off her hangover. But he wasn't about to share that little detail with the guys in this room. They would want to know how he knew that, and then they would inevitably draw the exactly correct conclusion. Frankly, it was none of their damned business how he and Chloe had spent the evening. Hell, even if he told them exactly what the two of them had done, these guys would never believe it. They would guffaw that quiet, controlled Chloe Jordan couldn't possibly be that wild.

Hah. Little did they know. He was a pretty adventurous guy in the sack, but that girl had made him blush a time or two last night. She was some woman.

"Maybe someone should go to her room and check on her," Jeff suggested, startling Trent out of recollections that were going to get him all hot and bothered very fast.

"Nah. I'm sure she's just sleeping. She was pretty wiped out last night."

"You walked her to her room and locked her inside sit?" Jeff asked.

"Yes. I searched her suite from top to bottom before I left. She clearly wasn't planning on going out again last night and was safe and sound when I left her."

Of course, she'd also been sexually sated and sleeping like the dead when he slipped out of her bed. She no doubt would need most of today to sleep off the booze and sex, though. A few of the things she'd asked for were going to leave her good and sore for a couple of days, but he'd been careful to do nothing she wouldn't recover from.

He wasn't sure he would recover anytime soon, though. How was any woman going to top that for him?

"Rather than bother her, couldn't we call her employer and ask for a list of companies she's investigated?" one of the twins, recent Code X additions with truly scary mental skills, suggested.

Trent shook his head. "She mentioned that she's a freelance consultant. I assume she contracts with law enforcement agencies or maybe banks. If we leave her a message, when she wakes up she can fire us a list of companies she has investigated." He desperately hoped his efforts to protect their little secret weren't rousing any suspicions.

Jeff nodded. "In the meantime, someone should keep an eye on her."

"As in surveillance?" Trent blurted, surprised. Damn. He'd been plotting ways to arrange a repeat of last night, but if the other guys were watching her around the clock, that was going to be hard to pull off. Unless he was the guy doing the surveillance...

"I'll keep an eye on her," he volunteered.

Jeff nodded. "I'll spell you when you need to sleep."

Speaking of which, it was about time for him to pop some sleeping pills and power down for a few hours. He might be able to go like the Energizer Bunny for days at a time, but when he crashed, he completely shut down. To that end, he commented, "I'm going to go catch a few zzz's now, so I'll be good to go tonight."

Jeff nodded. "I'll make a call to the concierge at her hotel. He can give us a heads-up if she leaves her room in the next few hours."

The powwow adjourned, and Trent headed for his own room. He showered again, popped his pills—a sleeping medication that would drop an elephant—and fell into bed. The soft sheets against his naked skin made him think of Chloe draped across him last night, and he fell asleep with a smile on his face.

Trent rolled over and glanced at the clock beside his bed. Six o'clock? Wow. He'd slept all day. Chloe'd tired him out more than he'd realized. Another side effect of his special abilities kicked in and his stomach growled loudly. He'd been known to burn in excess of twelve thousand calories a day when he was really active.

After ordering a steak, two baked potatoes, a large salad and a chocolate milkshake from room service, he moved over to his window to have a look across the street. Chloe's room was on the fourth floor, last one on the left. No light showed through the curtains. Given that Jeff had left no messages indicating that she'd left her room, she must still be sleeping off last night.

He probably shouldn't take satisfaction from that, but he couldn't help it. The idea of having made love to her until she had to sleep all day to recover made him smile. The last time he'd felt this kind of adolescent pride had been his first time with a girl when he was about sixteen.

A houseboy arrived with supper, and he pulled the wheeled cart over by the window to eat. His body eagerly absorbed the calories, and he eventually pushed back his empty plate in deep satisfaction. That should hold him for a few hours. He picked up a newspaper and browsed it while he kept an eye on Chloe's window.

Somewhere between the business and sports sections, her lights finally came on. Good thing. He was starting to get a little worried about her. About a half hour later, his cell phone rang. His pulse leaped as he dug the device out of his pocket. He was disappointed to see Jeff Winston's name on the phone.

"Hey, boss."

"Chloe just sent me a text. Turns out this Paradeo company is her first forensic accounting job. She says she's been hired to take a look at their books. Didn't say who hired her, so I assume she doesn't want to name her employer. We'll be in the conference room, researching Paradeo if you feel up to helping. You may have a long night tonight watching our girl, so don't feel like you have to come down."

"No problem. I slept and just finished eating. I'm on my way."

As the group researched Chloe's employer, nothing seemed out of the ordinary about it. Paradeo was a small-ish investment firm specializing in Central and South American markets. They reluctantly concluded that the Code X team might be forced to follow her and wait until another attempt was made on her life before they identified her attacker. Assuming there was one.

But Trent knew what he'd seen. That SUV had waited until she stepped into the street and then gone straight at her with the intent to seriously harm or kill her.

"Anybody know Chloe's travel schedule?" Jeff asked the room at large.

Novak's voice came across the speakerphone almost

immediately. "She's flying out of Denver Stapleton to-morrow morning. Arrives in San Francisco at 2:10 in the afternoon."

Jeff nodded. "We've got the manpower here to get her to Stapleton and onto that plane safely. Trent, if you want to go on ahead to California and get into position at the other end to take over watching her, that would be great."

He didn't like the idea of leaving her, even for a few hours. But what choice did he have? The odds were much greater that she'd be attacked at home rather than here where she was surrounded by Jeff and the rest of the Code X team.

Reluctantly, he packed his bags and headed for the late flight Novak arranged for him with Jeff's last warning ringing in his ears. "It would kill Sunny if anything hap-pened to her sister. And you know what's on the line if this thing turns out to be aimed at Code X. I'm counting on you, Trent."

One thing he knew for sure. Chloe Jordan was not get-ting hurt on his watch.

Chapter 3

Chloe inhaled the seaweed and fish smell of San Francisco Bay, and grief that never grew less painful washed over her. The scent reminded her painfully of living on the boat with her family for that last year, before Mom and Dad had left her and Sunny behind and sailed to their deaths in the Indian Ocean to protest commercial fishing practices decades before it was cool to do so.

It had been a mistake to take a job in this town. Too many memories lurked here, waiting to ambush her. Too much loss. Too many ghosts. This was the last place she'd been happy, innocent, carefree. But all of that was long gone.

Not that Denver was destined to fare much better in her memory. Her experience there had been an embarrassing anomaly in too many ways to count.

In spite of it being in San Francisco, she was glad to get back to her regularly scheduled life. Her orderly, quiet, controlled life. No more whiskey, no more drunk hookups, and no more unleashed fantasies.

She took a taxi to her modest apartment in a relatively quiet corner of downtown. Stepping into the spartan elegance of her modern Asian-fusion flat, she soaked in the calm of it. She hit Play on her phone's voice messages while she set about unpacking her things.

"Chloe, Don. We need to talk. Call me."

Don Fratello was the FBI agent-in-charge of the secret investigation into Paradeo Inc., a firm that was suspected of being a money laundering operation for a Mexican drug cartel. Despite her inexperience in forensic work, Don had cut her a break and given her a shot at this gig, for which she would be eternally grateful to him. It was nigh unto impossible to get hired without experience, and until she got hired for some jobs she couldn't get any experience. This chance he'd given her was a huge deal and she wasn't about to blow it.

She was working as quickly as she could on the case, but the firm used the most complicated accounting system she'd ever seen—a possible sign that Paradeo was playing fast and loose with where its dollars came from and went.

She put a load of laundry into the tiny washing machine that was one of her flat's best selling points and picked up the phone. "Hey, Don. It's Chloe."

"Are you back in town yet?" he demanded without preamble. "How was the kid sister's wedding?" he added as an obvious afterthought.

"Great. She's safely married off, and I'm a free woman now." She'd meant the comment as a joke, but what Trent said about her being alone in the world came back in a flash. A hot knife of pain twisted in her gut. Damn him, anyway.

"There've been a few developments at Paradeo since you left."

Interested, she replied, "Do tell."

"A new guy's been brought in. Name's Miguel Herrera. Title's Chief of Security. He looks like a major thug to me. My contacts south of the border have heard rumors of the guy strong-arming various judges and political officials."

"Which means what? You want me to target him specifically because he's a big fish?"

"No!" the FBI agent replied sharply. "Steer clear of him. This man could be dangerous. As in you disappear and never come back if he figures out what you're up to."

She highly doubted it was as bad as all that. This was San Francisco, for goodness' sake. Not some lawless Mexican frontier town.

"This guy could be a drug cartel hit man. If that's the case, he won't hesitate to kill you or worse."

"What's worse than being killed?" she asked.

"Trust me. You don't want to find out. Just be careful, okay?"

"Okay. I'll be careful."

She'd accuse Don of being a nervous Nellie if he wasn't an experienced FBI field agent. But if he was that uptight about Herrera, she'd take his advice and stay away from Paradeo's new security chief.

She hung up the phone and resumed listening to her messages. There were the usual hang-ups from telemarketers, a request for gently used clothing items for some charity, and then another male voice began to speak in hushed tones.

"Chloe? It's me, Barry Lind, from Paradeo."

Barry? She looked up, surprised, at her telephone. What was he doing calling her? He was a bookkeeper and did basic data-entry work for the firm. He was very good at his job but not particularly social with his coworkers. Chloe considered him at best a casual acquaintance.

His tense voice continued, "I didn't know who else to call. Can we meet somewhere to talk? Outside of the office. Call me as soon as you get this message."

Bingo. This was exactly the sort of break her professors had told her to look for during an investigation. The statistics were shocking as to how often the break came from a low-level worker. They always knew all the dirt.

Eagerly, she dialed the number Barry had left for her. "Hi, it's Chloe. I just got back into town and got your message—"

He cut her off sharply. "Can't talk now. Julio's after work? Say six o'clock?"

"Uhh, sure. I'll be there." Wow. He really sounded nervous. Her stomach leaped in anticipation. He must have stumbled onto something big. Perfect. The faster she took down Paradeo, the faster she could get away from thugs like this Miguel Herrera guy.

She unpacked, shopped, finished her laundry, and generally put her life in order while she waited for six o'clock to roll around. Finally, it was time to go. The streets were crowded at this time of day as workers poured out of their offices and headed for home.

Barry was waiting for her when she got there. His sandy brown buzz cut was distinctive in the shadows. The guy was not ex-military, but at a glance, someone might mistake his short hair and beefy build for that of an ex-Marine. He looked past her nervously as she slipped into the booth, predictably a dark one in the back corner.

"Hey, Barry. How are you?"

"I've been better," he muttered without moving his lips, his gaze sliding away from her and over her right shoulder. Wow. He was acting really nervous.

She smiled broadly. "A word of advice. If you act like a criminal with a big secret, people will watch you more closely. Relax. Try to look natural. No one's going to walk up to the table and shoot us."

"That's what you think," he grumbled. His hands were planted on the table like it was going to fly away if he didn't hold it down.

She reached a sympathetic hand out to him and gave his icy fingers a squeeze. "Tell me what's on your mind."

"So, yesterday I was working late. With the end of the quarter coming up and you out of town, we were behind." She nodded her understanding. "Anyway, I took a break to go to the bathroom. Except the one on our floor was closed for cleaning. No problem. I went upstairs to use the john." A sheen of sweat broke out on his upper lip, and he paused to mop at it with a cocktail napkin.

"So there I am, sitting on the can doing my business, and these guys walk in. And they're talking, see. In Spanish. My wife's from Mexico, and I've learned it from her over the years. Anyway, these two guys are talking about needing to destroy records."

"What kinds of records?" she prompted while he paused to mop his face again and grimaced.

"Financial records from Paradeo. They said there was this new accountant poking around and they had to get rid of the paper trail." His gaze darted toward the door yet again. Man, this guy was tense. And the feeling was contagious.

If Paradeo's executives were onto her, she would never get the dirt on them. They'd erase everything from the company's computers and she'd never find a trace of anything. She asked, "Who were the executives? Did you recognize their voices?"

"I think one of them was the new guy. Herrerra. Oh.

You haven't heard about him, yet, have you? New Chief of Security. Supposed to be a real hard-ass."

Crud. The last thing she needed was a violent killer suspicious of her.

"What did you do?" she asked Barry belatedly.

"I waited till they left, then I went back to my desk and I copied every last financial record I could lay my hands on in the company's computers."

Chloe gaped. "Are you serious?"

"Yup." He reached into his jacket pocket then laid his palm flat on the table and slid it toward her. "Take this," he muttered ventriloquist style.

She laid her hand over his and as he withdrew his, she felt the oblong shape of a flash drive. She palmed it unobtrusively and stuck it in the pocket of her jeans. "What do you want me to do with these files?"

"You are the new accountant they were talking about, right?"

"I suppose so."

"Then poke around and see what you can find, eh?"

She blinked, startled at how directly this guy was telling her to uncover the dirt in his company. "What do you have against Paradeo?"

His gaze hardened. "My wife is Mexican, remember? I have heard of Miguel Herrera's associates. If Paradeo is mixed up with animals like that, then the company needs to go down."

"Fair enough. I'll take a look at these files and see what we've got." She finished the soda the waitress left her and tried to engage Barry in small talk for long enough that it wouldn't look suspicious if she got up and left. But the guy was so freaked-out he couldn't follow the thread of even the simplest conversation. Eventually, she gave up and signaled for the bill. And all the while, that flash drive was burning a hole in her pocket. She couldn't *wait* to see what it revealed.

Trent fidgeted in the produce market across from some dive called Julio's. Who was the guy Chloe was with? He gnashed his teeth as she reached out again and touched the guy's hand across the table. Was that her boyfriend? He looked pretty normal. Could no doubt give Chloe a white picket fence and 2.2 kids and a Volvo station wagon. All the things Trent could never give a woman. His gut twisted in something resembling jealousy but a hundred times more painful.

Since when did this particular green monster bite him in the butt? He never cared who women slept with besides him. He'd always figured what was okay for him was okay for the women he had sex with, too. And it wasn't like he was looking for a permanent relationship complete with all the trappings. But Chloe…she had managed to blow his mind sufficiently that he might consider pursuing an actual, exclusive relationship with a woman like her. Okay, with her specifically.

But as that bastard in the bar leaned across the table to murmur something intimate to Chloe, Trent tasted for the first time the bitter gall of having been a one-night stand when he wanted to be more.

Had she played him? Was *she* the accomplished pickup artist who'd conned him into giving the hot sex she wanted and then walked away without a backward glance? He was pretty sure he could hear women laughing uproariously on several continents at this very moment.

And to think he'd been plotting ways to romance her, to sweep her off her feet and into a relationship with him. All the while, she'd just been using him. Damn, she had that vulnerable and lonely act down to a fine science. He could not believe he'd fallen for it!

Fuming, he moved to another vantage point inside the small grocery store he was using for surveillance. In this day and age, a guy couldn't lurk in a dark alley for too long without someone calling the cops. No one wanted a terrorist hanging out on their block.

"You gonna buy something, mister, or are you just fondling the fruit?"

Trent glanced down at the tiny Korean woman glaring up at him like he was some kind of pervert. "Yeah, sure. I'm buying." He threw a few bananas, a bunch of grapes and a container of cut, fresh pineapple into a small basket and shoved them at the woman. He hated leaving the window, but he had no choice. And he could do without seeing the bastard kiss Chloe. The way the guy was leaning across the table, he was gonna lay a big wet one on her any second.

Trent threw a couple of bills on the counter and waited impatiently for the proprietor to ring up his sale and count out his change. Hurriedly, he grabbed the plastic bag and headed for the front of the store.

Dammit! Chloe and Lover Boy were no longer at their table. Trent bolted out the grocery's front door and looked up and down the street frantically. There. Pale, golden hair in a flawless French twist. Relief made him faintly nauseous as he hurried after Chloe. She was almost a block ahead of him.

Not that he had any trouble catching up. Even at a walk, his extraordinarily quick reflexes allowed him to cover a lot of ground fast without really seeming to. Chloe crossed a street, but a changing traffic light forced him to wait at the corner. She opened up a gap with him again. But he had gotten close enough to realize with a start that Lover Boy was not with her. Where had he gotten off to?

Trent didn't know whether to be more relieved that Chloe hadn't gone home with the guy or worried that she was out strolling around after dark by herself when someone wanted to kill her.

The light changed and he pushed through the thinning foot traffic until he was within about fifty feet of her. She walked another three blocks or so and never once checked behind her to see if anyone was following her. Someone had to have a serious conversation with her about situational awareness. Of course, she probably had no idea that she was in danger, let alone the target of a would-be assassin. Despite Jeff's decision not to alarm Chloe until they had proof someone was trying to kill her, Trent was going to have that talk with her. Soon.

Although how he was supposed to just call her and casually bring up the fact that she was in mortal danger, he had no idea. Hell, she probably wouldn't pick up the phone if she knew it was him. Not after the way she'd taken advantage of him in Denver.

He was irritated enough that his attention lagged. One second she was in front of him, and the next, she was gone. Startled, he darted to the spot she'd been standing in a few seconds before. Where did she go? He was at the mouth of a dark alley full of trash Dumpsters and piles of bulging garbage bags. Several apartment buildings were nearby and she could have ducked into any one of them. Her place was still a half-dozen blocks away…maybe she was rendezvousing with the eager schmuck from Julio's.

Trent heard a muffled noise behind him and leaped into the alley. He made out violent movement in the gloom and a female form being dragged deeper into the alley by a much larger male form. A flash of pale hair caught what little light trickled in from the street.

His muscles coiled and sprang so fast he barely managed to control the motion. He regained his balance and his fist shot past Chloe's head to smash into her attacker's face almost too quickly for his eye to see the movement.

The mugger grunted and shoved her hard into the brick wall beside him. She cried out and her knees crumpled, but Trent had no time for her, yet. He threw punches at lightning speed until the mugger started to draw a weapon in slow motion from the back of his waistband. It was ridiculously easy to knock the weapon out of the guy's hand with a fast chopping blow. The guy's mouth opened slowly and his arm cocked back at what seemed to be about one-tenth that of normal speed.

Trent brought his right knee up as fast and hard as he could and slammed it into the guy's crotch. The attacker grunted and doubled over right into Trent's best uppercut. The guy went down like a rock.

Trent spun toward Chloe. She was slowly sliding down the wall toward the ground. He reached out, grabbed her shoulders and dragged her upright. She let out a squeak of terror.

"Chloe. It's me, Trent. You're safe now. I've got you."

She sagged against him, taking huge, sobbing breaths. He held her for a moment, registering for the first time the stench of the alley.

"Honey, I need you to stand up on your own for a minute, okay?"

She nodded against his chest but made no move to step away from him. He pushed her gently back against the wall and knelt down to check on the status of the attacker. The guy was out cold. He looked about thirty and was dark-

haired and scruffy. Might be Hispanic, maybe Mediter-
ranean. Hard to tell in the dark.

Trent reached into the guy's back pocket and whipped
out the attacker's wallet. He pulled out his own cell phone
and took a quick picture of the guy's driver's license. Trent
put the I.D. back and stuffed the wallet back in the man's
pants. He searched the guy's pockets for anything else that
might be informative and found nothing. He did pick up
the attacker's .38 pistol, which had skidded a half-dozen
feet away, and tucked it in his sweatshirt's front pocket.
If they got lucky, the gun might tell the guys at Winston
Ops who this yahoo worked for.

"Is that really you?" Chloe asked tentatively. "You're
not a hallucination?"

"Yup, I'm me. In the flesh." She looked like hell
warmed over. "C'mon, Chloe. Let's get you home."

"The police…arrest him…report…"

"I'll take care of it," Trent answered smoothly. He
pitched his voice to calm and reassure her. The last thing
he needed was police snooping around and asking too
many questions. Besides, the beating he'd administered
to her would-be assailant was a more effective deterrent
than anything the cops could do. However, it also opened
Trent up to some questions by the police that he'd really
rather not answer. Like how he was so fast, and had dis-
armed the assailant so easily, and why he didn't have a
scratch on him.

"I didn't recognize you in those clothes," Chloe commented randomly.

He glanced down at his jeans riding low on his hips
and his University of Hawaii hoodie sweatshirt. This was
what he usually wore. "What's wrong with my clothes?"
he asked.

"Nothing. I've only seen you in a tux or—" She broke off.

Or naked. He grinned down at her. If she could think about sex after having just been assaulted, she was going to be just fine once she got over the initial shock.

They walked the rest of the way to her place in silence. He watched without comment as she let herself into her apartment. But when she reached for a light switch, he forestalled her. "Stay here," he murmured.

She nodded as he slipped into the darkness and took a quick look around her place. It was as tidy as her hotel room had been. Its spare, modern furnishings left little or no room for someone to hide, and his search was complete in under a minute.

"Okay, Chloe. It's safe. You can turn on the lights."

A row of recessed halogen lights went on in the snug kitchen that was open to the living room. He watched cautiously as she dumped her coat on a bar stool and un-ceremoniously started stripping off her outer clothes in front of him.

"Whoa, there. What are you doing?" he asked in alarm. She wasn't going to jump his bones here and now, was she?

"I stink. I can smell him on me," she muttered.

And then he noticed her hands were shaking and she was unnaturally pale. In fact, her entire body was trembling. He moved to her swiftly and wrapped her in his arms. She went stiff against him.

"It's okay, honey. I've got you. You're safe. I swear. You can let it go, now."

She might have been close to tears in the alley, but she didn't break down like he expected. Instead, she pushed against his chest and he turned her loose, surprised. Where was the funny, relaxed, adventurous woman from two nights ago? Surely she was locked inside Chloe some-where.

"Turn your back," she ordered tightly.

He did so, frowning. He felt her move past him and head for the single bedroom that opened off the living room. The door closed with a thud and a lock snicked into place. She thought a lock would work against him, huh? He didn't disabuse her of the notion. All the guys at Code X learned how to pick nastier locks than her little bedroom door's as part of their extensive military-style training.

He sat down on her sofa to wait her out. He didn't buy for a minute that this tense, uptight woman was the real Chloe Jordan. She'd emerge eventually, and then they'd have that conversation about who might want to kill her.

Chloe scrubbed furiously at her skin under a scalding hot shower until it was red and felt raw. Whether she was trying to get rid of the feel of her attacker's arms or the feel of her rescuer's she couldn't say. Where in the heck had Trent Hollings come from, materializing out of nowhere to save her? He must have been following her. But why? Obviously, he was some kind of stalking creep. She couldn't believe he'd followed her from Denver all the way to San Francisco. Apparently his notion of playing for a living included terrorizing single women. Was he some kind of pervert?

An insidious thrill that he might have flown halfway across the country to see her again insinuated itself into the back of her brain. She tried to scrub it away, too, but failed.

After rinsing shampoo out of her hair for the third time, she gave up on getting any cleaner and stepped out of her shower. She felt horribly vulnerable being naked with Trent in the next room, and forewent her usual, meticulous drying and moisturizing ritual to hurry into clothes. She pulled on jeans and a bulky sweater that was the most concealing article of clothing she owned. She even put on socks and shoes. Anything to cover herself from *him*.

The humiliation of waking up stark naked in that hotel room and knowing he'd seen her—all of her—and done all those things to her, and that she had let him, was far too fresh in her mind.

She dried her hair and pushed it back from her face with a simple headband. In her efforts to delay facing him even further, she even applied a little makeup. Finally, when even her watch was strapped to her wrist and she couldn't think of a single thing more to do, she gathered the rest of her filthy clothing in her arms.

Oh, God. The flash drive. The mugger had groped her coat pockets—no doubt looking for her wallet. She didn't remember if the guy had reached into her pants pockets, though. She'd been too panicked to register such details.

Chloe reached frantically into the pocket of her jeans and felt a hard rectangle of plastic. Exhaling in relief, she tucked the drive into her underwear drawer. It wasn't the most original hiding place ever, but it would do until she could get rid of Trent Hollings and make a bunch of copies of the data files. And she wasn't giving him permission to go fishing through her lingerie anytime soon.

Steeling herself to face the devil, she opened her bedroom door and stepped into the living room. As she'd expected, he was still sprawled on her sofa, waiting. In that baggy sweatshirt and tennis shoes with his hair all tousled, he looked like an overgrown kid. She could barely believe he'd been the dark, dangerous lover of two nights ago.

"Feel better?" he asked neutrally.

"Yes, thank you," she answered equally neutrally. Lord, she barely recognized him like this with that tousled hair, sloppy clothes and dark stubble on his jaw. He looked nothing like the wealthy trust-fund playboy he apparently was. He reminded her of some surfer-dude, hippie throwback of her parents' days. Ugh. She much preferred him in an Italian designer tuxedo.

She bustled over to the closet by the front door that hid her washing machine and stuffed her smelly clothes into it. She doubted they would ever be wearable again, but getting that awful stench out of them felt therapeutic, at any rate.

Too nervous to be still, she moved into the kitchen and poured herself a big glass of water. Although it annoyed her to do it, she poured Trent one, as well. Just because he was a possible stalker didn't mean she could bring herself to be rude, particularly when he was behaving himself so well at the moment. It just wasn't in her nature. And that darned thrill in the back of her head kept doing backflips that he was here.

She set his water down on the glass coffee table in front of him. He picked it up and sipped at it without comment. At a loss for anything else to do, she sat down on the matching chair across from him. "Thank you for rescuing me…again," she started stiffly.

"My pleasure. But let's not make this a habit, eh?"

Her gaze snapped up to his. "Do you have reason to believe there will be more occasions in which I need saving?"

"Yes, actually. I do. And we need to talk about that."

She stared at him. "You think the SUV in Denver and that mugger are related? Wow. And I thought I was paranoid."

"You have an enemy, Chloe. And he or she could be rich and powerful. Given the frequency and violence of these attacks, that person is very angry at you."

She frowned. "But this is my first real gig as a forensic accountant. And I haven't found anything that could convict Paradeo's senior executives, yet."

"That doesn't negate the fact that you're the person who could uncover the evidence to put them in jail."

"If not me, someone else would do it."

"Still, you have no business strolling around a big city like this at night, alone, enemies or no enemies."

"What business is it of yours how I live my life, anyway? It's my life."

"True. But your sister loves you a great deal. She'd be devastated if anything happened to you."

That was a low blow, invoking her sister. "And why do you give a darn about Sunny's state of mind?" she snapped.

"Why *don't* you?" he shot back.

She recoiled, offended. "I think you should leave. Now."

"Sorry. I'm not done talking, and you really need to hear what I have to say," he retorted grimly.

She gauged the distance to the phone on her kitchen counter. She would never make it across the living room and get 911 dialed before he reached her. She'd seen his reflexes firsthand in the alley, and although she was pretty out of it after her head hit the wall, he had moved in a blur of speed.

He shoved a hand through his hair. A pang of memory, of the lust provoked by that hand on her body, speared through her. Fine. She admitted it. He was still as handsome as ever. And sexy, darn him. And his smile was still as charming when he said, "This conversation got off on the wrong foot. How about we start over?"

Her eyes narrowed skeptically, but she made no comment. He could talk all he wanted. It was his breath to waste.

"Sunny married my good friend and colleague, and that makes her family. Which, by extension, makes you family, too. If for no other reason than that, I would be concerned for your safety. Additionally, in spite of what you seem to think, I consider you and I to have a...connection...after Saturday night."

"Do not *ever* speak of that again," she gritted out from behind abruptly clenched teeth.

He frowned as if he'd like to argue the point with her, but then continued plowing through whatever twisted logic he was pursuing. "The fact remains that I am worried about your safety. And so is Jeff Winston. He asked me to keep an eye on you until we can figure out who's trying to—" he paused as if stopping himself from saying something too revealing "—who might be trying to harm you," he finished lamely.

"Harm me?" she exclaimed.

"You said yourself that the SUV in Denver came out of nowhere. I heard its engine gun. And there were no skid marks, Chloe. That vehicle was accelerating toward you."

She shrugged. "The driver probably didn't see me."

He leaned forward, his intense silver gaze altogether too sexy and distracting. "Then why didn't he stop or even slow down when he nearly hit you? I guarantee you, had I not knocked you out of the way, he would have hit you, and you would have died."

"Are you implying that the driver was trying to kill me?"

"I'm not implying anything. I'm telling you outright that's how it is." He leaned back once more in a casual sprawl across her sofa that left her abruptly short on oxygen. Did he have to be so blessed attractive?

"That's crazy," she declared forcefully.

He sighed. "I figured you'd feel that way. I was hoping not to have this conversation until I had solid proof. But that guy in the alley forced my hand."

"So you were planning to follow me around without my

knowledge and spy on me indefinitely while you gathered this hypothetical proof?"

Chagrin crossed his features, but then a cajoling twinkle in his eyes took over, making him look even more boyish than ever. "I'm not spying on you. Think of it as me providing security. Good thing, too. Who knows what that jerk in the alley would have done to you if I hadn't been there."

"I'd have gotten his hand off my mouth and screamed my head off, and someone would have come to the rescue."

Trent snorted. "That guy was a lot bigger and stronger than you. Don't kid yourself. He'd have done exactly what he wanted to with you long before the police could come to the rescue, no matter how fast they responded."

A chill chattered down her spine. Was Trent right? Had she really come that close to disaster? Surely not. She announced, "I don't buy your conspiracy theory. Muggings are an everyday occurrence in big cities. And as for that car in Denver, the driver had probably been drinking and didn't want to stick around in case I called the cops on him."

"You're determined not to believe me, aren't you?"

"Pretty much."

"I'm going to keep digging until I get the proof I need to convince you."

Crud! She really didn't need him following her around and tipping off Herrera and his cronies that something was odd about her. Trent would totally mess up her investigation if he persisted with this little delusion of his.

The first order of business was to get rid of him and his boyish smile and magnetic charm. The second was to call his boss and have a chat with the man. Jeff Winston struck her as eminently reasonable. He would call off this obsessive lackey. "Fine. Whatever. Please leave and don't bother me again."

"Bother you? I'm trying to save your life!"

"Whatever makes you feel like a hero. Just keep your distance from me or I'll call the police."

He opened his mouth. Shut it. Stood up. Took a single step toward the door, then turned to face her. "For the record, my being here has nothing whatsoever to do with Saturday night. I've had hot lays before and I've never followed any of them around to save them from their own misguided ignorance."

Her jaw dropped in outrage, but before she could gather herself to tell him in no uncertain terms what a giant jackass he was, he was out the door. Dang, that man could move fast.

So furious she nearly flung his glass of water across the room, she squeezed her fingers into fists until they hurt. How did Trent keep getting under her skin? Call her ignorant, would he? She definitely hated him. Passionately.

Yup, the man had passion down to a fine science. And as memory of the things he'd done with her flashed through her mind, she groaned with a different kind of passion. The man was as irritating as sand between her toes.

Not about to waste another minute on him, she picked up her phone and dialed Jeff Winston's number.

"Winston Ops. Go ahead."

"This is Chloe Jordan. I'd like to speak to Jeff Winston, please."

"One moment, please" the smooth female voice said, "while I check to see if he can take your call."

While she waited for the secretary or whoever it was to return to the line, she opened up the laptop on her counter and typed in Jeff Winston's name. She was till absorbing the shock of the long list of companies he and his grandfather owned and the total cash value it represented when the female voice returned. "One moment for Mr. Winston."

"Hi, Chloe. This is Jeff. Is everything okay?"

"Yes. Fine. Except I have a little problem with an employee of yours. This may sound strange, but I think he's stalking me."

"Are we talking about Trent Hollings?"

"Yes. Does he have a history of this sort of behavior?" she asked in relief.

Jeff laughed. "Hardly. Women chase him like crazy, but he never gives them the time of day."

"Well, he's following me."

"I know. I told him to."

"Excuse me?"

"Sunny is family now, and so are you. I sent Trent to keep an eye on you until we can figure out who might want to, umm, bother you."

"You mean kill me?" she retorted.

"I'm not sure I'd go that far," he demurred with patent insincerity. Jeff Winston obviously believed someone was out to kill her, too. She tuned back in to what he was saying.

"…wouldn't want to unduly alarm you, Chloe. But my people pulled footage from a traffic camera in Denver, and that SUV appeared to be targeting you specifically," he finished delicately.

"It was a fluke. Or the driver mistook me for his ex-wife, or he didn't see me. I don't know what Trent thinks he saw, but the man's delusional."

Jeff replied gently, "The vehicle idled with its engine running for nearly an hour in its parking spot. But the moment you exited the club, it pulled out into the street. It waited in place for you to start across. When you did, it accelerated directly at you. I hate to alarm you, but Trent wasn't mistaken."

She didn't know what to say to that.

"Look. He'll stay out of your way. I can put a full surveillance team on you if you'd like, but I thought you might be more comfortable having someone you know do the job. Plus, Trent will be a little more unobtrusive than a large team of operatives."

She swore mentally. An entire team of security men trailing her around was the *last* thing she needed. No way would Herrera miss something that obvious. And if this hypothetical security team was as ham-handed as Trent in its approach, it would surely succeed in wrecking her case and maybe getting her killed. Like it or not, Trent Hollings was the lesser of two evils.

"Really, Jeff. I don't need any protection. I'll be just fine." God, why couldn't her life ever be normal?

"With all due respect, Chloe, I'm not convinced. Tell you what. If Trent watches you for a couple of weeks and there are no more incidents, I'll pull him off the job and never bug you again."

It wasn't a great compromise, but it was better than nothing. And as long as Trent kept his distance, she supposed she could tolerate a few weeks of knowing he was watching her. Although the mere notion of him checking out her every move sent shivers through her. *Yeah, but what kind of shivers?* A little voice murmured in the back of her head.

Not *those* kind! she shouted back at herself. "Fine," she grumbled. "Two weeks. And then he's out of here."

"Deal. Pleasure doing business with you, Chloe."

Was that laughter in his voice? Why did she suddenly

feel like she'd played right into his hands? Nope, she didn't like Jeff Winston much more than his incredibly annoying employee.

Chapter 4

Chloe spent the remainder of the evening making multiple copies of all the files on Barry's flash drive. She burned them to a CD, saved them to her online file storage account and, most importantly, forwarded them to Don Fratello. He couldn't read even the simplest financial statement and would expect her to do the heavy lifting in analyzing the files, but this way the FBI had a backup copy. And their computers were super secure.

She took a cursory glance at the files, and it looked like Barry had grabbed a complete record of Paradeo's activities for the past several years. It would take days or even weeks to plow through all the information, but if there was a money trail buried in here, she would find it.

The physical stress of travel and the emotional stress of being attacked had exhausted her, though, and eager as she was to dig into Barry's files, she turned in early. Her professors always stressed that a case like this was a marathon, not a sprint. She had to pace herself if she wanted to stay sharp.

The next morning, she stumbled through her usual routine by rote, showering, dressing and eating breakfast with blessed normalcy. She kept a sharp eye peeled for Trent as she headed for work but never spotted him. She didn't know which was creepier: seeing him following her or not seeing him at all. At least he was keeping up Jeff's end of the bargain and staying out of her way. She made her way to Paradeo's offices on the fifth floor of a downtown office building and spent most of the morning digging through the minor crises that had piled up on her desk in her absence.

It was nearly 11:00 a.m. before she was able to make her way past Barry's cubicle without being obvious about it. She poked her head in to thank him for the gift and to give him a quick thumbs-up regarding the completeness of the content. But when she looked around the corner, he wasn't at his desk. His computer was turned off and no papers cluttered his desk. Which was strange, come to think of it. His desk was normally messy enough that she had to restrain an urge to straighten it.

She asked his supervisor in the cubby next door, "Have you seen Barry, today?"

"No. He didn't come in to work. And," the woman added tartly, "he didn't call me to tell me he was sick, either."

"Okay. I'll catch up with him tomorrow." Something didn't feel right in Chloe's gut. Barry hadn't been sick last night when she saw him. And now that the files were out of his possession, he had nothing to worry about. He should've been at work today and acting as if nothing was wrong. Trent's paranoia was contagious, darn him! Barry had probably spent the morning in bed sleeping off his stress or maybe a hangover.

At lunch, she left the office and bought herself a salad at the deli down the street. She called Barry's cell phone number to check on him, but got no answer. Her unease intensified. And speaking of which, where was her own personal ball and chain? She searched up and down the block for a tall, gorgeous physique in the crowd. No sign of Trent. But she swore she could feel his gaze on her. It was almost a physical caress in its intensity. No doubt about it, he was there even if she couldn't see him. If only he didn't make her skin tingle like that!

Aww, c'mon. Admit it, Self. You like knowing he's looking out for you.

That little voice in the back of her head could just go take a hike. She went back to work and threw herself into finishing her piece of the quarterly report, which took the rest of the day. At quitting time, she had about an hour's worth of work left to do on the thing and decided to stay late and finish it. Not to mention doing so would probably irritate the heck out of Trent.

The office emptied and the phones quit ringing. As silence settled around her, she focused intently on the columns of numbers on her computer screen. One more footnote to post on a one-time charge as required by law, and she'd be done.

"Chloe Jordan?" a heavy male voice said in her doorway.

She looked up at a man she'd never seen before. "Can I help you?"

"I'm Miguel Herrera. New Chief of Security."

She swore to herself. Way to go avoiding the guy who'd be most likely to stick around late and lock the place up. Dumb, dumb, dumb. Pasting on a polite smile, she moved around her desk to shake hands with him. He was about her height and powerful in build. His neck was thick and muscular, and she had no doubt that under his suit the rest of him was equally beefy. "Glad to have you here, sir. Now I'm not the newest kid on the block anymore."

Herrera smiled, but the expression never touched his cold, black eyes. She got the distinct feeling he was mentally calculating the best way to dissect her into Chihuahua-food-sized kibbles. "How much longer will you be here this evening, Miss Jordan?"

"I'm just finishing up the quarterly report. Two more minutes, tops."

Herrera gave her a long, assessing look like he was measuring the truth of her explanation, and she restrained an urge to squirm. "Next time you plan to stay late, tell me first," he finally growled.

"Of course." He left her office and she sagged in relief. The guy really did reek of contained violence. No wonder Don had warned her away from this guy. More eager than ever to get home and dig into Barry's files, she hurried through the last footnote, sent her data to Paradeo's Chief Financial Officer and headed home.

She didn't bother looking for Trent when she stepped out of her building. She was in too big a hurry to get away from Herrera's disturbing presence. When she had to walk past the alley where the man had jumped her the night before, she couldn't help herself. She swung wide of the dark gap, edging along the parked cars and hurrying her steps.

Thank goodness Trent had been there last night. As much as she might resent his intrusion into her life, who knew what that mugger really would've done to her? In a moment of brutal honesty, she allowed reluctantly that Trent probably hadn't deserved her generally rude response to him last night. It wasn't his fault she'd gotten drunk and found out the hard way what a floozy she was on whiskey. She was embarrassed, but that wasn't his problem.

Thankfully, she'd left a lamp on in her apartment this morning and didn't have to step into a dark space. She kicked off her high-heeled shoes gratefully. Visions of a red stiletto flying over a broad, sexy shoulder came unbidden to her mind.

Get out of my head! Echoes of rich male laughter were the only reply her mind offered up.

To drown the memory of Trent's voice urging her not to overthink, to let go and show him just how naughty she could be, she turned on the television. Local news blared as she moved into the kitchen to whip up dinner for herself. The act of chopping and stir-frying a wokful of cashew chicken calmed her.

She poured herself a glass of chardonnay and moved into the living room to relax while the rice steamed. The news anchor's voice caught her attention. "And in local news, accountant Barry Lind was found dead in his apartment this afternoon, the apparent victim of a robbery gone wrong…"

Her wineglass slipped from her fingers and crashed to the floor, shattering on the slate tiles.

Gut-twisting fear slammed into her harder than Trent Hollings had on that street in Denver. She collapsed on the couch, staring at the television in horror as it flashed a picture of Barry that looked a few years old and declared his death a tragic loss. The reporter moved on unconcernedly to the next story as if he hadn't just destroyed her world.

Her front door knob rattled and she scrambled to her feet in terror, stumbling on the edge of the area rug as she backed away from the door. A snick and the knob turned. Ohgod, ohgod.... Someone was breaking in. She was next to die—

She spun and ran for her bedroom. A hard, powerful arm snagged her around the waist from behind, yanking her back against a muscular body. She screamed and a big hand slapped across her mouth.

"Easy, Chloe. It's me. What the hell's going on? Why did you freak out like that?"

She nearly sobbed aloud in relief as Trent's deep voice rumbled in her ear. His hand lifted off her mouth. His body was big and warm and protective plastered against her back, and an urge to sink into him and let him take care of her came over her. But then anger erupted inside her. "You scared me to death!" she exclaimed.

He turned her in his arms, but infuriatingly didn't let her go. Or to be more accurate, she was glad he didn't turn her loose, and *that* made her furious with herself.

"Me?" Trent exclaimed. "You were completely terrified by something long before I got here. I saw you drop your wineglass and go as white as a sheet. That's when I hoofed it over here as fast as I could."

How had he seen her? She glanced over at her picture windows in chagrin. She'd always been claustrophobic and preferred to leave the blinds open to the city view.

"Chloe? What's going on?" he urged.

His question pulled her back to Barry's tragic fate. "He's dead," she mumbled as tears started to flow down her cheeks.

"Who?" Trent's voice was sharp now and his hands tightened on her shoulders.

"Barry. The guy I met for drinks last night."

"Your boyfriend?" Trent's voice changed tenor. "Oh, honey. I'm so sorry." He wrapped his arms around her and drew her against his big, comforting chest.

"He's not my boyfriend. He is…was…" her voice cracked "…an accountant where I work. He wanted to talk over a problem he was having at work."

"What kind of problem?"

Not the kind that she was prepared to discuss with anyone but Don. "Just some accounting stuff," she replied evasively.

"How did Barry die?" She couldn't fail to hear the charged anticipation in Trent's voice. He didn't seriously think Barry's death was related to her, did he?

"The news said he was murdered at home possibly confronting a robber."

Trent frowned, but didn't comment as he pulled out his cell phone and plastered it to his ear. While he waited for someone to come on the line, he used his free arm to guide her over to the sofa. He sank down onto it and pulled her down beside him, never removing his arm from around her. Whether she liked it or not, he held her practically lying across his chest.

In spite of how frustrated she was at having him shadowing her life, she had to admit his body heat and slow, steady heartbeat were both comforting and calming. What the heck. She gave up resisting his superior strength and relaxed against him, accepting the comfort he was offering. His hand stroked her hair absently. She would have purred like a contented cat if the man who'd stolen sensitive data and passed it to her hadn't just been killed.

"Jeff, it's Trent. Coworker of Chloe's was killed today. She met him for drinks last night to talk about work stuff and he was murdered in his home overnight."

She faintly heard Jeff's reply. "I'll send a full team right away."

"No!" she exclaimed, struggling to push upright on Trent's chest. "No team!"

"Honey, you're in grave danger," Trent replied soothingly. "We need the extra manpower to protect you."

"I can't have an entire security team trailing me around. It'll ruin everything!"

Trent answered whatever Jeff said with, "Nope. No idea what she's talking about. Yeah, I'll find out. We can't exactly force her to cooperate with us."

She stared at Trent in dismay and mouthed again, "No team!"

He frowned at her while he listened to Jeff. He said only, "Got it. I'll be in touch." And then he disconnected the call.

Trent stared down at the exasperating woman trapped against his chest. Single-handedly protecting her from killers was a tall order. And he *really* didn't want to see anything bad happen to her. He had plans for the two of them.

"Will you please explain to me why don't you want a team of highly trained field operatives to keep you alive, Chloe?"

"I can't."

"Can't or won't?"

"Same difference."

He sighed. "Look. I'm one of the good guys. I'm trying to help you, but you're making it damned hard to do."

"I don't need your help."

"I beg to differ. Twice now, someone has tried to harm or kill you, and your colleague, to whom you must have been one of the last people he spoke with, is dead. Wake up and smell the coffee. You're in real danger."

She stared at him a long time, her eyes as big and blue as the sky on a clear day. Emotions washed through her azure gaze, one after another. Distrust. Doubt. Frustration.

And finally, fear. Relief flowed through him. At last, she was getting past her denial enough to believe him.

But then she said, "I've been in rough situations before. I'll be okay."

"Not this time. Whoever's coming after you is violent and proficient."

"They can't be that proficient. I'm still alive."

"Because I've been around to save you," he snapped. And he'd succeeded in protecting her both times by the skin of his teeth. "Pretty soon, your would-be killer is going to start figuring me into the equation, and I won't be enough to keep you safe any more." His arm tightened protectively around her.

Her flash of defiance faded. "What am I supposed to do?"

"Let me help you. Let Jeff and a full-blown security team help you."

She was silent a long time. Finally, reluctantly, she said, "All right. But no team. Just you."

"I can't be everywhere at once. You'll be safer with a full security detail."

"I might be safer, but it would ruin my investigation. It's you or nobody."

He sensed that was her final offer. But he didn't like it. "What or who, exactly, are you investigating?"

Chagrin washed across her face. "I assume you followed me to work today and figured out which company I'm working for."

"I did," he answered evenly. "And where are you in your investigation with Paradeo?"

She hesitated, and then capitulated and spoke in a rush. "Barry gave me a flash drive with a bunch of financial information on it. That's why he wanted to meet me last night."

"Were they worth killing over?"

She stared at him, appalled. "You think that's why Barry was killed?"

He shrugged. "Hard to tell." He didn't want to suggest that mere contact with her could have been enough to cause a motivated killer to go after Barry. She would never get over the guilt of it.

"So how do we do this?" she asked.

An image of her naked and tied up beneath him flashed through his head. Startled, he shook it off and forced his mind to work. "I'm going to be glued to your side from now on. I'll figure out who's after you and, when the bastard shows himself, I'll catch him and turn him over to the authorities. Then you can resume your regularly scheduled life. In the meantime, you should take some time off work."

"I can't. The FBI has hired me to investigate Paradeo, and I have to see it through."

"Not if it's going to kill you."

She sighed. "A certain amount of risk is part of the job."

"Not this much risk," he retorted. "You've got Barry's files here at your place, don't you?"

"Well, yes."

"Then you can work on them at home."

"But it will raise suspicion if I suddenly disappear from Paradeo. And, I don't know if Barry got the entire goods on the company. If he didn't, I may still need access to the company's financial records. And that means keeping my job and the appearance of normalcy for a little longer."

He didn't like it one bit, but he could see her point. "I'm still staying glued to your side," he declared.

"You can't exactly sit beside my desk all day long without raising serious red flags with my superiors," she replied, alarmed.

Dammit, another good point. "No, but I can drop you off at work and pick you up, and I can watch you in your office from across the street."

She frowned. "I suppose I could live with that."

He wasn't giving her a choice in the matter, but he refrained from sharing that particular detail with her. She was finally letting down her guard with him, and he wasn't about to raise her hackles again unnecessarily.

"Where do you keep a broom?" he asked.

"Excuse me?"

"If you'll get a towel to mop up the wine, I'll sweep up the broken glass."

She fetched him a broom and dustpan. As she disappeared into her bedroom in search of a towel, he raced through cleaning up the glass. He was done by the time she got back.

"Man, you're fast," she commented. "How did you do that?"

He swore at himself mentally. He would have to be more careful not to give away his special ability. "It wasn't that big a job."

But her frown suggested she didn't entirely believe him. To distract her, he asked, "What's that delicious smell coming from your kitchen. Have you eaten yet?"

"It's cashew chicken. And, no, I haven't. Have you?"

He winced. "I should warn you. I'm pretty much always hungry."

"Good thing I made a big batch, then."

After a delicious supper, he called Winston Ops. "Hey, it's Trent. Has Jeff briefed you on the latest from here? Good. Can you get a hold of the police report and find out what their preliminary guess is as to how Barry died?"

He only had to wait a minute or so. How on earth Winston's people got access to the San Francisco police department's database so quickly, he hadn't the slightest idea. Frankly, he didn't want to know. The favors Jeff was able to call in on a moment's notice were scary.

Novak announced, "Death by strangulation with a metal wire. Looks like your guy was garroted."

Trent grimaced. That was the method of a professional killer. Quiet, fast and effective.

Novak added, "We I.D.ed the guy from the alley last night. Mexican national, crossed over into the U.S. as recently as a week ago. Rap sheet in Mexico a mile long. But all his arrests stopped about a year ago."

"Police bought off to leave him alone?" Trent bit out.

"Looks like it. If he's involved with one of the powerful drug cartels, they'd have the power to get the *Federalés* off his back. We're still working on which cartel he's hooked up with."

"Thanks. Keep me updated, will you?" He ended the call.

"Well?" Chloe demanded.

"Well what?"

"How did Barry die?"

"He appears to have been murdered." She didn't need to know all the gory details; she was already upset enough. "How about I do the dishes so you can take a peek at those files Barry gave you?"

She nodded and disappeared into her bedroom. When her kitchen sparkled, he dried his hands and strolled into her bedroom to check on her. She sat at her desk, concentrating fiercely on her laptop screen.

Her apartment had about as much personality as a wet sock. Odd how so passionate a woman was so restrained in expressing herself. Her bathroom was as bland and neat as the rest of her place. He opened her closet and wasn't surprised to find a row of boring suits. He checked over his shoulder to make sure she wasn't paying attention to him and opened her drawers one by one. Nothing. No sign of the woman he'd made love with in Denver. Her socks and panties were as practical and uninspired as everything else in this place. Clearly, Chloe Jordan needed whiskey soon and often to break out of this shell she'd locked herself inside.

He stretched out on her bed and read a newspaper for the next hour. Finally, she pushed her chair back and raised her arms over her head in a stretch. He rolled off the bed and moved behind her. Yup, that knot in her neck he'd felt in Denver was back. He dug his thumbs into it and smiled as she groaned her pleasure.

"Taking a break or finished for the evening?" he murmured.

"Just a break," she moaned, her head rolling forward.

"Have you got any whiskey?"

She stiffened beneath his hand. Whoops. There was the knot again. "Why?" she asked cautiously

"Because you need to loosen up. Bad."

She turned in her seat to face him. "Let's get one thing straight. You are here to protect me. Nothing more."

"I never agreed to that," he retorted.

"Then I'm making it a new condition. This is just business. Purely professional."

"Sorry. No deal."

For a moment, she looked like she was seriously considering going along with his implied indecent proposition. But then her expression closed and her gaze went hard. "Excuse me?" she said ominously.

"You heard me. I make no promises to keep our relationship platonic."

"We don't have a relationship!" she exclaimed.

"I'm sorry. Have you forgotten Saturday night? As I recall, we have one hell of a relationship."

Her cheeks turned red. "That was…an anomaly."

"You can call it whatever you want, honey. That was the hottest sex I've had with anyone in a long damned time. Maybe ever. And I plan to do it again with you."

Her jaw dropped. "Never."

"Is that a challenge?" he asked softly. If she knew him better, she'd recognize the note of danger in his voice. But apparently, she didn't know him that well, yet.

"No, Trent. It's a promise. I'll never do that again with you."

"Ahh, you shouldn't have said that. I never could walk away from a dare."

Chapter 5

Chloe stared up at Trent in dismay. One of his hands still rested lightly on her neck, and electric shocks zinged outward from his palm and straight to her core. The rational half of her mind was appalled at his declaration. But the other half of her mind was thrilled, darn it.

Reason kicked in again. She didn't know the first thing about this man. And establishing her career left no time for relationships. Not to mention he was so beautiful she would always feel like a second-class citizen around him. He would leave her eventually. Everyone did. She could do without the heartbreak. Most important of all, she was terrified by how he made her lose control.

Mmm. But that's the best part, her emotional self murmured.

No. It was not.

Wanna bet? her wanton self retorted. *Tell him about the*

bottle of whiskey in the liquor cabinet in the living room and see what happens.

She steeled herself for whatever assault he planned to launch against her resistance, but he surprised her by stepping away from her and saying only, "I'll let you get back to work."

Stunned, she watched his yummy back retreat into the living room. She definitely hadn't expected him to back off that easily. Was he not all that attracted to her in spite of his big talk of bedding her again?

Hurt at the notion, she turned her attention back to the financial data in front of her and resumed her analysis. Or she tried to. But every time she wrote down a new column of numbers she ended up staring at it and making no sense of it whatsoever. Instead she kept seeing Trent's glorious body looming above hers. His face tight with desire and his eyes dark with need that she had put there.

As she added up a list of numbers for the third time and came up with a third different total, she gave up and threw down her pen. She stormed out into the living room to confront the source of her distraction. "I can't get a darned thing done, and it's all your fault."

He looked up from the book he'd borrowed from her shelves. She noted vaguely that the self-avowed beach bum with no job was reading an advanced tome on economic theory. Did he actually understand it, or was he just trying to impress her?

"How can I make it better?" he asked mildly.

He could scratch the itch he'd planted in her head, darn it. She opened her mouth to make a snappy comeback. Closed it. No way was she going to admit she was attracted to him. It was a passing thing. He was a hot guy and basic biology dictated that she would react. It was nothing personal and nothing she planned to do anything about.

She stomped into the kitchen and made herself a mug of herbal tea. Belatedly, she offered, "Tea?"

"Only if it's decaf."

"Do you have trouble sleeping?" Rats. Her curiosity to know about this man slipped out before she could corral it.

He shrugged. "I usually have to take medication to go unconscious. And those drugs don't mix well with caffeine."

"The way I hear it, sleeping pills can be habit-forming."

"They are."

"Have you tried to kick them?"

He smiled but his eyes remained closed. Secretive. "I really can't sleep without help. It's a metabolism thing."

Which also explained his comment about being hungry all the time. She sipped her tea and let its smooth flavor soothe her.

"So what's your story?" Trent asked her.

The question surprised her. He actually wanted to know more about her than how she behaved when drunk?

"You've seen my life. Work. Accounting. My apartment."

He frowned. "Hobbies? Interests?"

"No time."

"Friends?"

"A few. We go out to dinner now and then."

"Boyfriend?"

"Again, no time."

"That's a lie."

His statement startled her. It also offended her a little. Maybe because he was partially right. Other people, including her sister, were fond of telling her she needed to make time for a relationship. She might just make time for a man like Trent Hollings—

Horrified, she broke off the train of thought. That man

was way out of her class. Not to mention he'd break her heart as sure as she was sitting here.

"Why don't you want a boyfriend, Chloe?"

He asked the question in a conversational tone, but she didn't miss the intensity underlying it. "I'm not gay, if that's what you're implying," she retorted.

He laughed. "I already had that one figured out. I was there Saturday, remember?"

She rolled her eyes at him. "I really wish you'd quit talking about that. It was…" She didn't know quite how to describe it.

"It was what?"

She scowled. "A one-time aberration." She couldn't quite bring herself to call it a mistake. But she did declare, "It will never happen again."

"I think you're about three shots of whiskey away from a repeat performance. And I also happen to think you wouldn't mind that so much. Furthermore, I think you need a repeat performance."

"And that's why I've sworn off drinking for good," she snapped.

"Are you telling me I've ruined you for all other men? Why, Chloe, I'm flattered."

Her scowl deepened while his grin widened. "What say we head for bed?" he suggested casually.

She bolted to her feet, alarmed. "This isn't going to work. You need to leave—"

He cut her off gently. "I don't sleep, remember? I was suggesting that you go to sleep while I keep an eye on things. Out here. In the living room."

"Oh." And didn't she just feel silly. She turned away from the glint of humor in his striking silver gaze and stalked into her bedroom.

She locked the door, but immediately, his voice floated

through the panel. "You might want to leave that unlocked. If I have to get in there in a hurry to protect you, I'd hate to have to break the thing down. Better if I can get in straight away."

Disgruntled, she unlocked the door without opening it. A faint chuckle was audible and she stuck her tongue out at him from behind the safety of the door. It felt weird taking off her clothes knowing he was just outside, and she raced into the T-shirt and sweatpants she usually slept in.

She pulled the covers up to her ears and squeezed her eyes shut, but nothing could close out the memory of his hands on her skin or the wanton things he'd done to her. Things she'd craved. Begged for, even. She pulled a pillow over her head and groaned beneath it. If only he'd just go away and leave her alone!

Or else come in here and do all of those things again that had set her blood on fire and made her feel truly alive for the first time in a very long time.

Trent sat in the dark, listening to Chloe toss and turn in her bed. Trouble sleeping, huh? Thinking about him and their night together, perchance? He smiled into the night. His plan to seduce the good Miss Jordan was proceeding very nicely. She'd been so distracted tonight she could hardly see straight. And her gaze had kept straying to his mouth, his chest, his hands. Remembering the feel of him, was she? Like any good predator, he was patient. She would come to him and beg for a repeat performance even if he had to pour whiskey down her throat to get her to admit she wanted him. He'd already discovered her liquor cabinet, and it happened to contain an unopened bottle of a decent single malt Scotch whiskey. Yes, indeed. The good Miss Jordan was going to be his. It was just a matter of time.

* * *

Chloe woke with a start to the sound of her shower running. She jolted upright and then remembered. Trent. The water turned off and she slid down under her covers hastily. The bathroom door opened and he stepped out in a cloud of steam wearing…oh, God…a towel. Slung casually around his hips and showing off intensely male abs and a heck of a nice tan. Lots and lots of nice tan.

"Did I wake you? Sorry," he murmured.

"My alarm clock was about to go off anyway," she mumbled.

"Any requests for breakfast?"

"I usually have a cup of coffee and a bagel."

"I need something more substantial. You get ready for work and I'll cook."

She stepped into her bathroom and stopped cold. His clothes were strewn on the floor, the bath mat soaking wet with his footprints in it. There were specks of shaving cream on the wall of her shower, the things on her counter misplaced. It was like a tornado had blown through her bathroom. Heck, through her life. And he wondered why she had no interest in dating. Hah.

She piled his clothes in the corner, scrubbed down her shower, and put her shampoo, shaving cream and toothpaste back in an orderly row from tallest to shortest. There. Order restored. She showered, vividly aware that Trent had just been in this very spot, naked, with hot water sluicing over his body the same as it was doing over hers. More heated than her shower could account for, she dried off, dressed and twisted her hair into its usual knot at the back of her head.

As she applied mascara, she became aware of the most amazing scent emanating from her kitchen. "What are you making?" she called out.

"Scrambled eggs and crêpes suzette."

"For breakfast? Isn't that a dessert?"

He called back, "Crêpes are skinny pancakes. Strawberry's a fruit and whipped cream is a dairy product. Sounds like breakfast food to me."

She smiled beneath the lip gloss applicator. She checked her appearance one last time and froze. Since when did she put this much care into getting ready for work? Since Trent Hollings blasted into her life. She stepped out into the main room.

"Hey, beautiful." He smiled. "Fresh batch of crêpes is up. I ate all the eggs. Sorry." He put a plate on the breakfast bar for her beside a glass of fresh-squeezed orange juice, and she slid onto a stool, stunned. Two perfect crêpes oozing sliced strawberries and nestled in a blanket of whipped cream sat on her plate. "My God, these look fabulous."

"I like to cook. Since I eat so much, it seemed like a reasonable skill to master."

She took a bite and groaned in delight.

Trent grinned in satisfaction. "I'm glad to see you allow yourself at least a little pleasure."

She looked up sharply. "I beg your pardon?"

"You seem bent on denying yourself any happiness in life."

"I am not."

"Had me fooled."

Her frown deepened.

"So you often have wild sex with men you barely know, then?" he asked with deceptive mildness.

"No," she blurted, "I don't. Ever. I wasn't kidding when I said you were an anomaly."

"In my experience," he commented reflectively as he rolled four more crêpes and placed them on a plate for himself, "Very little in life is random. There's a reason you chose me to let down your hair with. I wonder what it is."

Truth was, he was the only man who'd really seen her at that wedding. Most men looked right through her like she wasn't even there. And he'd been safe. She was never going to see him again. Ships passing in the night, and all. She snorted mentally. That sure hadn't worked out the way she'd expected.

Trent's plate was already nearly empty. "How do you do that?" she demanded.

"Do what?"

"You do everything so fast."

His gaze was abruptly guarded. "I guess I'm just efficient."

"I leave the room for a few seconds, and when I return you've done ten times as much as I expected."

"Maybe you're just lazy."

Were it not for the glint of humor in his eyes, she might have been offended. As it was, she laughed. He smiled back and her breath hitched. He was so handsome he was hard to look at sometimes. Under other circumstances, it would be very easy to fall for a man like him. Of course, a man like him would never fall for a girl like her for real. He might have enjoyed the hot sex, but he would never really care for her. They were too different.

"What?" Trent asked suddenly.

She frowned, confused.

"You got this strange look on your face just now. If I didn't know better, I'd call it wistful. What were you thinking?"

"How different you and I are."

"How's that?"

"Well, you're the original blue-blooded playboy. I come from the exact opposite," she answered.

"Tell me about it."

"Trust me. You don't want to hear about it."

"I wouldn't have asked if I didn't want to know."

No way was she spilling all the sordid details of her dysfunctional life in front of this perfect man. She leaned over the counter to set her plate in the sink. Retreating from the dangerous topic of conversation, she collected her laptop and briefcase from the bedroom.

And he did it again. By the time she got back, the dishes were done. Efficient, her foot. That man must move at supersonic speed to get things done like he did. He glanced up at her innocently. "Ready to go?"

She nodded, frowning, and waited just inside the door when he gestured for her to let him go first.

"Hall's clear," he announced.

The streets were jammed with cars and bicycles. She boarded her usual streetcar and Trent angled his body between her and the other commuters, but it pressed him against her from shoulder to knee. He ended up wrapping one arm around her and hanging on to the overhead bar with his free hand. On cue, her breath shortened and her pulse accelerated.

Of course, Trent didn't miss a thing and smirked down at her. Jerk. He knew exactly the effect he had on her. The streetcar swayed and rattled, throwing her against him. His arm tightened, steadying her and pressing her a little closer against his amazing physique.

She tried to hold herself upright, to put a millimeter or two between them, but it was a complete failure. The car lurched again and plastered her against him. The stupid streetcar was never going to get to her stop!

But finally, her office approached, and she was stunned to feel regret as Trent stepped away and ushered her down the steps and onto the street. However, he kept one arm possessively across her shoulders and her glued to his side.

They had to look strange, her in a gray pin-striped business suit with matching pumps and her hair in a perfect up-do, and him unshaven and in his sloppy sweatshirt. Still, many women, and even a few guys, threw her envious glances.

Warmth spread through her. It was nice having a hunk like Trent publicly stake a claim on her. She checked herself sharply. She knew better than to fall for him. Caring about anyone was a sure recipe for driving that person out of her life.

Trent insisted on walking her into her building and actually depositing her at her desk. The other women in the accounting department made no bones about their appreciation for her escort.

"Who's the gorgeous hunk, Chloe?"

"Wow. Introduce me to his brother, will you?"

Some of the women just muttered things like, "Hubba, hubba."

Trent took it all with good grace. He must be used to that sort of reaction. As he lifted her purse off her shoulder, she grumbled, "The minute you leave they're going to interrogate me. What am I supposed to tell them?"

"Stick to the truth as much as possible. Tell them we met at your sister's wedding and hooked up. I was so blown away I followed you back to California."

"Excuse me?" she blurted.

He grinned broadly. "They'll think it's unbearably romantic and eat it up. Trust me. I know women."

Her body tingled instantly in response. He did, indeed, know women. She would never forget how well.

"I'll be across the street watching you. If you need me, just wave and I'll be here in a flash."

Her prediction turned out to be true. She barely got any work done all morning as women kept poking their heads in her door to demand the scoop on the pretty man-toy. She did tell them she'd met Trent at Sunny's wedding, but she left out the bit about him being blown away and following her back to San Francisco.

Yet another shadow darkened her office door and she glanced up, irritated. Whoops. *Miguel Herrera.* Her entire body tensed. "Can I help you?" she finally remembered to ask.

"I hear you were friendly with Barry Lind."

Alarm bells clanged wildly in her head. "I knew him. I don't know that I'd describe him as a friend," she replied cautiously.

"Did you see him before he died?" Herrera asked, watching her with an intensity that missed nothing.

Trent's reminder to stick to the truth as much as possible came to mind. "Let's see. I saw him last Wednesday before I left for my sister's wedding at the progress meeting for the quarterly report. He seemed fine."

"You didn't see him after you got back?"

What did this guy know? And how was she supposed to explain that meeting in the bar? She hedged, "Yesterday was my first day back to work. And he wasn't here—" Her voice broke. "Do they know what happened, yet? Was it a robbery gone bad like the news said?"

"He was garroted. Murder. Head was damn near cut off," Herrera answered bluntly.

She gaped, genuinely appalled. "That's horrible." Tears came to her eyes at the thought of Barry dying like that. Was it her fault in some way? Had this man discovered Barry's copying of the files and killed him for it? Her gaze strayed to the window in distress.

Herrera stared at her hard enough that she had to stop

herself from squirming. He made her feel like a guilty kid caught with her hand in the cookie jar. "You sure you don't know anything that could shed some light on his murder?" he demanded.

Oh, God. He did know something. Why else would he be pushing her like this? Panic clawed at her rib cage from the inside, desperate to burst out and send her fleeing from this man who could very well be Barry's killer. She stammered something inane and prayed Herrera would put down her reaction to shock.

"Hey there, beautiful."

The security man whirled, his hand twitching toward his hip.

Trent. How did he know? One second she was wishing for him to rescue her, and practically the next, here he was. She smiled at him in abject relief as he strolled past Herrera, whose hand was inching away from his hip slowly. She leaned into Trent as he reached her side and kissed her cheek. His arm slipped around her shoulders.

"And who's this?" Trent asked.

She mumbled through the introductions, and Herrera left quickly. She started to express her relief, but Trent quickly pressed a finger against her lips.

"I know it's a bit early for lunch, Chloe, but I want to take you somewhere special. Can you leave now?"

"Uhh, yes. I guess. My part of the quarterly report was just approved."

"Great. Let's go."

They were settled in a cab before Trent turned to her, expression grim. "Who the hell was that guy, and why did he put that scared look on your face?"

"Miguel Herrera. New Chief of Security."

"He's a dangerous man."

"Good eye. He may be linked to a drug cartel."

"Hence the FBI's interest in your employer. Do they think the firm's laundering drug money?"

She threw an alarmed look at the back of the cabdriver's head. Trent caught the hint and changed subjects. "I'm taking you to my favorite place in town to eat."

"It looks like we're headed for the docks."

"We are."

Chloe winced. The waterfront was fraught with memories she'd rather not face. Not to mention it was a pretty rough section of town. Not a place she belonged. She wasn't reassured when the cab stopped at the back of a disreputable-looking fish market. Exactly the sort of place her parents would have loved. The old embarrassment poured through her as if she were nine again. Her folks had been free spirits with no regard for social convention or propriety. They'd called such notions authoritarian repression of the masses.

Trent helped her out of the cab and banged on an unmarked door. It opened to reveal what could only be termed a dive. The dark room was full of rough-looking men in rough clothes bellied up to a bar where a rough-looking guy served up cheap plastic baskets overflowing with batter-fried fish and chips.

She could hear Mom and Pop crowing in delight now…a gathering place for the Working Man. Yup, her parents would've smoked enough weed to lose what little common sense they had and barged right into a place like this.

Speaking of which, "Trent, should we be here?" she murmured under her breath. "We don't exactly fit in."

"You don't, maybe. Stick with me, and you'll be fine."

Not reassuring. Particularly when whistles and catcalls announced that everyone in the joint had noticed her.

"What is this place?" she muttered. "Some kind of biker bar?"

"Something like that," he answered cheerfully. He elbowed them a spot at the bar and yelled a hello down the bar to the proprietor, who bellowed back, referring to Trent by name.

"You're a regular, here?" she demanded under the din.

He shrugged. "I know a few people here and there."

How on earth did a guy who came from his kind of money even find a place like this?

Trent yelled for two lunch specials, which were served up almost immediately. The fish was hot and flaky, the fries thin and crispy, just the way she liked them. She reluctantly had to admit the food was delicious. But she had worked her tail off to get as far away from this side of the tracks as she could. She wanted middle-class suburbia. Ozzie and Harriet Nelson. The Brady Bunch.

Trent, surprisingly, seemed entirely at ease. She had to admit his size and general roughness of dress and shave weren't all that out of place. Gradually, she relaxed enough to finish her lunch.

Still, she breathed a sigh of relief as they stepped outside without any brawls breaking out. She hurried away from the wharf, eager to leave behind the blast from her past.

"You really are a bum, then?" she asked him.

He glanced over his shoulder at the fish bar. "I like places like that, if that's what you mean."

"Why?" she asked, shuddering.

"The people are real. Not trying to be something they're not." He looked at her in surprise. "Why don't you like a place like that? You said yourself the food's fantastic."

"My parents dragged me to places like that and worse. I've worked my whole adult life to leave that world behind and make a better life for myself."

"And a better life means what? More money? Fancy

clothes? Shiny, clean places and shiny, happy, *fake* people?"

She stopped and turned to face him. "You don't seriously mean to tell me you prefer that squalor to, say, the gentlemen's club in Denver!"

"I'd absolutely rather hang out with a bunch of fishermen in some rat hole than with a bunch of snooty, blue-blooded hypocrites in some fancy club."

He was crazy.

"Why do you have such an aversion to that sort of place?" Trent challenged. "Why do you love the trappings of wealth so much?"

"I have no interest in dredging up my past," she replied tightly.

They hiked a little while in silence as they approached a street that a brave cabbie might venture down. Thank goodness her heels were low and her pumps fit perfectly.

He spoke casually and his steps sped up a little, "I can always have Winston Ops run a full background check on you. They'll tell me exactly why you don't like working-class places and where your obsession with money comes from."

"You wouldn't," she exclaimed, appalled.

"Either you tell me, or I'll find out for myself." He was walking noticeably faster now.

"That's an invasion of privacy!"

"We pretty well blew up any notions of privacy between us in Denver. I figure that night gives me the right to know." He glanced around as if seeking a cab. But no yellow sedans were in sight.

"I wish that night had never happened."

Something pained passed through his crystalline gaze. He covered it up with a crooked smile, but she didn't buy it. "Aww, you don't mean that, baby."

"Yes, I do," she declared.

He turned with that breathtaking speed of his and swept her up against him. Before she could draw a breath his mouth closed over hers. His kiss was carnal. Knowing. He invaded her mouth with his tongue, his arm a vise that smashed her against him without any pretense of polite restraint. He knew her most private desires and fantasies, knew she craved being overpowered from time to time, and he didn't hesitate to remind her of it.

It was no use resisting him. He knew her too well. He exerted the same mastery over her body and senses that he had that fateful night, branding her his all over again. And she melted. Again. She'd asked for a man to take charge of her and take her to the moon, and he had. It was still there. All of it. The fiery attraction. The flare of mutual passion. The synergy that built between them until it incinerated her soul.

He let her go as abruptly as he'd kissed her. "No. You don't," he declared quietly.

Huh? Her fuddled mind reached back for the thread of conversation he'd scorched clean out of her mind. Oh. She'd said she wished that night had never happened. *Okay, fine,* she told herself bitterly. She didn't wish that. But she was never, ever, going to admit it to him.

Trent resumed walking, and she stumbled, trying to keep up with his long stride. "Slow down," she finally panted.

"Sorry. Can't. We're being followed. Hold my arm if that'll help."

She grabbed his elbow and let him half drag her along at a near run. She didn't see anyone behind them, and Trent muttered an order at her to quit looking.

Scared and desperately trying to distract herself, she picked up the thread of the conversation. "Sunny said you're from a—I believe her word was stupidly—*wealthy* family." His jaw tightened but he made no comment. She continued. "So tell me this. Why do you hate money so much?"

He stopped briefly at the first busy intersection they came to and made a production of adjusting her purse strap on her shoulder. She noticed him surreptitiously watching behind her while he was at it.

"Is he still there?" she asked between her teeth.

"Yup."

"Now what?" she asked nervously.

"We're going to run. Now."

"Huh?"

"Run."

Chapter 6

Chloe did her best to keep pace with Trent as he took off running, but it was a stretch. They careened around a corner and Trent darted out into the street, dragging her along, to hail a cab. He shoved her inside and bit out instructions to the cabbie. She was stunned when he slammed the door shut on her and took off running back the way they'd just come.

The cab started to move.

"Wait!" she cried out.

"The guy said to take care of you, lady."

"But he's in danger. We can't leave him behind!"

"He told me to get you out of here."

She looked out the rearview window and there was no sign of Trent. She had no clue where he'd darted off to. "Somebody was following us. I can't just abandon my friend. Would you at least circle the block once so we can check on him? You don't have to stop. *Please*."

The cabbie relented, and the taxi turned the corner. She stared in shock at the sight that met her. A man was fleeing from Trent. But what dropped her jaw was how *fast* Trent was catching up. He looked like a track star. On steroids. In fast-forward video. The guy Trent was chasing looked like he was running in slow motion by comparison.

"Whoa. That guy can move. He a professional athlete or something?" the driver exclaimed.

"Or something. Follow him, will you?" Chloe directed the driver.

The cabbie had to punch the gas pretty hard to catch up with Trent. The guy he was chasing veered around a corner and Trent disappeared as he darted around the corner, too. By the time the cab got to the intersection, both the fleeing tail and Trent were gone. The cabbie circled the block again, but Chloe didn't glimpse Trent or the man he was chasing.

"They must've ducked inside a building," the driver announced.

She leaned back against the cracked vinyl cushions, perplexed. How did Trent move so fast? If he was that amazing an athlete, why wasn't he a professional sports star? "Thanks for trying," she told the cabbie in defeat.

"Okey dokey, miss. I'm taking you home, now."

She fretted the entire ride back to her place. Was Trent all right? Why on earth was he chasing after that guy? What if Trent's quarry turned out to be one of the bad guys and he turned on Trent? She realized with a start that she'd wrung her hands until they were bright red. She jammed them under her thighs to keep them still.

She paid the cabbie, tipped him generously for his help, and hurried up to her apartment. Funny how exposed she felt without Trent around to look out for her. How had he managed to worm his way into her life in one lousy day? Although she supposed it was a day-and-a-half if she counted Denver.

She double-checked the locks on her apartment and wielded an umbrella like a sword as she searched her place for intruders. Satisfied that she was home alone, she took the unusual step of closing the blinds. Distracted, she called the office to let them know she'd be working from home this afternoon. She tried to look at Barry's financial files, but she had the focus of a gnat.

Where was Trent? Should she call the police? She didn't even have his cell phone number to call him and check on him. But Jeff Winston would have it. She raced to her phone and called Winston Ops.

"Novak here. Go."

"Hi. It's Chloe Jordan. I need to get in touch with Trent Hollings."

"Turn around and talk to him," Novak replied jokingly. Then more seriously, "Isn't he with you, ma'am?"

"No. He chased after some guy who was following us and sent me home alone. I don't know if he's all right. It's been nearly an hour since I last saw him."

"Stand by." Abruptly the operations man was all business.

She waited in an agony of impatience. Trent had to be okay. He just *had* to.

"I'm tracking his cell phone and it is on the move. That doesn't mean he's with the device, however. He's not answering at the moment. Protocol is to give him thirty minutes to respond before we call the police."

"Oh, God." Something had happened to him. She knew she shouldn't have left him!

"Don't worry, Miss Jordan. Trent's one of our most experienced operatives. He can take care of himself. I'm sure he's fine. I'll call you back as soon as I know something."

And in the meantime, the clock was ticking down on something being very, very wrong.

Trent leaned back, badly rattled, in the cab as it lurched in fits and starts across San Francisco's crowded, construction-filled streets. Now why would that guy kill himself rather than let Trent question him? He'd only shouted out one question—the obvious one—to the tail as the guy ran out of room in the warehouse and crouched defensively in the corner. *Who are you?*

The guy had shaken his head, muttered back at him in Spanish and then reached inside his jacket.

Trent had tensed and coiled his body to jump at full speed to avoid being shot, but instead the poor bastard had jammed the barrel of the gun in his mouth and blown his own brains out. Shock had, for once, literally frozen Trent into immobility. And the mess had been incredible. His guts twisted into an awful knot. Had he not chased the guy, he'd still be alive. But the dude had definitely been following him and Chloe. He seriously hadn't been planning to hurt the guy. He'd just wanted to know whom the tail worked for.

Trent had snapped pictures of the body from across the warehouse and hoped the resolution was high enough that the wizards at Winston Ops could do something with the images. Maybe they could identify the poor kid.

If he was lucky, he'd left no forensic evidence behind for the police to find. It wasn't that he minded talking to the authorities, but right now he really had to get back to Chloe to check on her. If he knew her, she was losing her mind.

What kind of organization put its employees under orders to kill themselves before allowing themselves to be questioned?

He hopped out of the cab a few blocks from Chloe's

place and hoofed it the rest of the way back. No sense leaving an easy trail for anyone to follow. He paused for a moment in front of her apartment door to mentally gird himself for the next looming crisis. He'd glimpsed her cab following him earlier as he ran at full speed. He hoped the angle had been such that Chloe didn't get a good look at just how fast he was moving, but he feared that hadn't been the case.

He never showed civilians his true abilities. It raised too many questions with highly classified and controversial answers. The dead man's incredulous last words echoed in his mind… "What are you? Some kind of monster?"

That was him. A twenty-first century Frankenstein monster. And on that grim note, he knocked on Chloe's door.

"Who's there?" a quavering voice asked through the panel.

"It's me. Trent."

The door flew open and a blonde, fast-moving object launched itself at him. He grunted as Chloe's weight slammed into him, and he used her momentum to spin them through the door. He kicked it shut with his foot while Chloe wrapped her arms around his neck and all but choked him. Damn, but he was glad to see her, too. He'd hated being away from her, even for that short time.

"Miss me?" he asked wryly.

"I was so scared. And you disappeared and we couldn't find you and I called Winston Ops and they couldn't get a hold of you and—"

He cut her off gently. "I was worried about you, too." He showed her how much by kissing her. And hoo baby, did she kiss him back. Recognition exploded across his brain. *Here she was.* The passionate, unrestrained, expressive woman had finally broken through.

Her hands moved across his chest frantically as if she were checking to make sure each and every rib was intact. Her fingers passed across his neck, his jaw, his cheekbones and through his hair.

"Really. I'm fine," he murmured against her mouth. Warmth unfolded inside him at the depth of her concern.

"Don't leave me again," she begged.

"Well, okay then." He laughed against her lips. Her hands went under his sweatshirt and she groaned in what sounded suspiciously like unbridled lust. She shoved the soft garment over his head as he guided her toward the sofa. He let her push him down onto it, amused at her urgency. She tugged at his waist, and his belt slithered free of its loops. Then her hands were on his zipper.

As much as he wanted this, he was an honorable man. He didn't take advantage of scared, vulnerable women. He caught her wrists and asked, "Are you sure about this?"

Her answer was to yank down his jeans and throw a leg across his hips. He'd take that as a yes.

It took every bit of his nimble hand speed to divest her of her clothes while she literally crawled all over him, kissing him and nipping at his flesh until he was nearly as frantic as she. What was it about this woman that drove him completely out of his mind? Was it the contrast between the conservative, uptight accountant persona she showed the world and this private, passionate part of herself she only shared with him? Whatever it was, she lit a fire in him like no other woman had.

She impaled herself on him eagerly, and rational thought fled in a groan as pleasure ripped from his throat. He surged up into her tight heat, gripping her hips and pulling her down to meet him. She leaned back as if she were a wild creature riding an untamed bronco. And he bucked beneath her just like one as she drove him completely out of his mind.

They rolled off the couch and crashed to the floor laughing, never breaking the furious rhythm of their lovemaking, pushing each other into oblivion and beyond. Her lust unleashed was a sight to behold as her entire body flushed, straining toward him. She keened her pleasure, throbbing around him so sweetly that she flung him over the edge, as well. He rolled over, pinning her beneath him, and continued to drive into her as his body recovered without pause and demanded yet more of her.

Chloe's eyes glazed over as she lost herself in him, shuddering again and again against him and around him until, with a shout, he joined her in spasms that rocked his entire body again.

They collapsed together in a boneless heap and let the floor's cold slate gradually quench the fire between them. Finally, with a groan, he rolled over onto his back and drew her on top of him. With his metabolism, he was rarely cold, but she'd begun to shiver. "Better?" he asked.

"Mmm. Much."

"Convinced I'm unharmed?"

"Mmm-hmm."

She sounded like a contented kitten on the verge of passing out. He smiled into her hair. She did have a knack for making a man feel like the king of the world.

A faint buzzing sound from nearby interrupted their lazy relaxation, and he reached for his wadded trousers. He dug out his cell phone. "Yes?"

"There you are," Novak said in relief. "I was about to send the cavalry after you. Chloe's frantic."

"I'm with her now. It's all good. But the guy I was chasing blew his brains out rather than tell me who he worked for."

Chloe tensed against him abruptly. He sat up dismayed as she climbed to her feet, snatched up her discarded clothes and fled for her bedroom.

"I've got a picture of the guy," he told Novak. "Not sure how good it is, but I'll send it to you. Maybe you can I.D. him and figure out who he worked for." They ended the call and he duly sent the image from his phone to Winston Ops.

And now for damage control. He sighed, climbed to his feet and headed for Chloe's room. He had no doubt she would retreat into her cold, cautious persona the same way she did after the first time they'd made love. How could he convince her she had nothing to be ashamed of? That her wild passion was something to be proud of?

As he stepped into her bedroom, she yanked an oversize pillow sham off her bed and held it in front of herself. He skipped mentioning that he had a great view of her entire naked backside in the mirror behind her.

"For God's sake, put on some clothes!" she screeched.

"Why? It's not like you haven't seen me in all my glory a few times, now."

"It's embarrassing!"

He grinned. "After the things we've done together? We just had hot monkey sex on your living room floor."

"You don't have to remind me," she snapped. She did, in fact, look completely mortified.

Yup. The prude was back. He perched a hip on her dresser and crossed his arms as she scurried around grabbing clothes and yanking them on. "Tell me something, Chloe. Why do you pull this hot-and-cold routine?"

She whirled to glare at him. "I'm never hot. At least whenever you're not around."

She spat the last bit at him as if it were a dire accusation. He grinned unrepentantly. "Good thing I'm going to be around for a while then, eh?"

"No! This sucks!"

He intercepted her as she rushed past him in an apparent search for shoes, snagging her around her slender waist and pulling her close.

"Let me go. And for God's sake, put some clothes on."

"Relax, Chloe. I'm not going to tie you up and ravish you…at least not unless you ask for it again."

Her face reddened. "You're really a jerk, you know that?"

He kissed the tip of her nose. "I have heard that before. But the past half hour tells me you don't really believe it."

"Oooh!" she ground out.

"When are you going to get over this irrational fear of your own sensuality? It's nothing to be ashamed of. You should be proud of your capacity for giving and receiving pleasure. Embracc it. Enjoy it."

"Never," she ground out.

"Why not?" He stared down at her, genuinely interested in her answer.

"I already told you. I don't come from the same background you do."

"Honey, women from every walk of life are equally capable of enjoying sex. Why are you so tense about it?"

"I just want a normal, boring, everyday life. Not a life like yours."

What the hell was so weird about his life? Okay, so he could run like the wind. And he never slept. And there was the money, of course… Dammit, his life *was* weird. He stated matter-of-factly, "Fine. If you won't tell me about yourself, I'll have Novak run a deep background check."

"No!"

He looked her in the eyes and saw genuine panic.

"I want to know, Chloe. If you won't tell me, I'll find out some other way. But I'm done with you giving me emotional whiplash. Since it's clear Denver was not, in fact, a one-time thing, I'm going to have to insist that you share at least a few of your secrets with me."

"Why?" she all but wailed.

"Because I want to know you. All of you. Not just your body. I want to know what you like. Don't like. What you think about. What makes you tick."

"But why?" she repeated.

"Because it's part of having a relationship. I happen to like you, Einstein."

She just stared. He couldn't tell if it was shock or sheer, frozen terror immobilizing her like that. Eventually she thawed enough to grumble, "Fine. Then tell me how it is you can run that fast. How is it you do everything so freakishly fast?"

She *had* seen him running. He turned her loose and shoved a hand through his hair. Now what the hell was he supposed to do? He had a serious security breach on his hands. Maybe if he played it cool she wouldn't realize just how incredible what she'd witnessed was. Panic squeezed him as he stared down at her, silently pleading for her to not to comprehend what she'd seen.

"That's what I thought. You want to know all my secrets, but you aren't about to give up any of yours," she stated.

He swore under his breath as he marched into the living room to retrieve his clothes and pull them on. They weren't his secrets to tell. But he couldn't even explain that much to Chloe. In spite of the earlier chase and the more recent vigorous sex, he really felt a need to work out. Adrenaline was surging through his veins demanding release. And that meant he needed to move. Faster than he could move in her living room. It was a calculated risk to leave her alone. But it would take a brazen killer to break into her place with the lights on and the target wide awake and able to fight back. And he'd be no good to her at all if he didn't burn off a little of this steam.

She was so damned frustrating. She claimed to want a normal relationship but balked at sharing even the most basic information about herself. It was as if she was so terrified of losing control that she had to hold all the cards between them to herself. What kind of normal was that?

Of course, the one thing he absolutely, positively couldn't ever give her was normal. Not with his health complications. He was probably stuck taking the stem cell therapies for the rest of his life. Unless, of course, he wanted to die a slow and horrible wasting death from spinal muscular atrophy. Not.

Hell, depending on how their genes matched up, they might or might not be able to have children. The good news was the recessive gene for SMA was reasonably rare.

And then there was his work. It had seemed like a waste to have these incredible physical abilities and not put them to good use helping mankind. He'd never guessed he would take such satisfaction in the work. He and his Code X colleagues were quietly making the world a better place.

However, the constant travel and no-notice crisis responses made a normal home life pretty much an impossibility. It would take a special woman to live with his whacky health issues and whackier lifestyle. Someone who embraced weird. Not a woman who craved "normal" worse than life itself.

He'd finally met a girl he could see himself settling down with for a long time, and he was *all* wrong for her. If this was God's idea of a joke, the big guy had a *lousy* sense of humor.

He announced from the living room, "I'm going out for a little while."

Chloe appeared in her bedroom door immediately, looking worried. "I thought you weren't going to leave me alone again."

What the hell? One second she was screeching at him to get away from her, and the next she was giving him this kicked-puppy look and begging him to stay? She officially made him crazy.

Reaching behind his waist, he pulled a .38 revolver out of its concealed holster and laid it on the coffee table. "Do you know how to use one of these?"

"Don Fratello said every woman should know how to handle a gun, and he made me take a weapons safety class," she answered.

"Who's Don Fratello?"

"The guy from the FBI who hired me. He's an agent in the financial crimes unit."

Trent didn't like the affectionate look that came into her eyes when she spoke of the guy, but at least she knew how to use a gun. He growled, "My friends Mr. Smith and Mr. Wesson will keep you company while I'm gone." He was so jumpy he could hardly control himself as he headed for the door. "I'll be back in an hour or two."

"You did it again," she accused. "How do you move that fast?"

"I just do." And with that lame excuse, he let himself out and pulled the door shut behind him. He waited until he heard the dead bolts thrown home and then raced for the stairwell. He needed a major run in the worst way right now.

Rather than risk drawing attention to himself by sprinting up and down San Francisco's crowded thoroughfares, he took a cab to an exclusive health club that had private workout rooms for rent by the hour.

He cranked the room's treadmill up to full speed, which wasn't anywhere near as fast as he could run, but it was better than nothing. He jogged along at fifteen miles per hour until the jittery feeling left his limbs. Lord, that woman messed him up.

He showered and dressed, then took a cab to the hotel room he'd been using to watch Chloe's apartment across the street. Quickly, he packed the gear and clothes he would need for the next few days, and fatigue abruptly began to drag at his body. That was how it was with him. He went ninety miles an hour until he hit the wall. And then he crashed like a big dog.

Forcing himself to keep moving, he stopped by a small grocery store and stocked up on food. And then he carried the entire armload of luggage and grocery bags down the street to Chloe's building.

She let him in as soon as he identified himself, although this homecoming completely lacked the same… enthusiasm…as last time.

"What's all that?" she asked cautiously.

"Clothes and surveillance gear. And food for the next day or two. Until we know who that guy was that followed us today, I don't want you to go outside."

"But my work—"

"You just caught the flu. And you can use the time to study Barry's files, right?"

She scowled but didn't argue. As he put away the food, she retreated into her bedroom and sat down in front of her laptop. It was clear she planned to immerse herself in the files and have nothing to do with him for a good long time. Which was just as well. He could hardly focus his eyes.

He moved over to her door and leaned against the frame. "Chloe, I need to sleep for a while."

"Fine. Take a nap."

"Uhh, that's not quite how it works with me. I'm going to take a sleeping pill and crash for the next several hours."

"Okay," she replied, distracted, already turning her attention to the columns of numbers in front of her.

She still didn't get it. "I'm going to sleep like the dead. Nothing you do will rouse me and don't bother trying. Keep that pistol close by and be prepared to defend yourself if someone breaks in."

That got her undivided attention. "You wouldn't wake up even if someone tried to kill me?" she asked in disbelief.

"Nope. When I go down, I go completely down."

"Several hours, you say?"

He shrugged. "I might sleep for as much as six hours. I haven't slept for a couple of days."

"A couple of days!" she exclaimed.

Rather than try to explain the unexplainable, he backed out her door and headed for his bags and his bottle of pills. He started as her voice came from directly behind him. "What are those? Superstrength Xanax?"

"Something like that." In point of fact, the medication was a custom blend of powerful sleeping medications and a surgical anesthesia drug. The doctors running the Code X program hadn't found any other remedy for his intractable insomnia so far.

He popped the pill dry and kicked off his shoes. Chloe came back with a blanket and a pillow for him as he stretched out on the couch. She handed them over, murmuring, "Sweet dreams."

He plumped the pillow under his head as the medication began to have its effect, and he gratefully sank into its embrace. He replied groggily, "If I dream about you, they will be."

As Trent passed out, Chloe retreated into her bedroom and breathed a sigh of relief. Facing him after today's epic mistake on her living room floor was one of the hardest things she'd ever done. It had been bad enough to have hot sex with the man when she was under the influence. But this time...this time she had no excuse at all. She'd jumped that man like a complete hussy, and she'd been stone-cold sober.

She laid her head down on her desk in humiliation and self-loathing. She was not that kind of woman! In the hippie, free-love world she'd spent her childhood exposed to, she'd seen plenty of people happy to jump in the sack with anybody who came along. She'd always promised herself she would be different. Modest and respectable. How did that old adage go? Square parents raised round children, and round parents raised square children? She was a square, darn it. She was *not* round!

Trent brought out a side of her she'd vowed never, ever to let gain control of her. She was not a captive of passion, was not following in her parents' disastrous footsteps! She would control her life, and she would *not* cave in to these base desires Trent roused in her.

No more slips. He was strictly hands-off from now on. But a sinking feeling in the pit of her stomach warned her the promise was going to be a lot harder to keep than it sounded.

She took a hot shower, attempting to scrub the feel of his hands and lips off her skin with the scratchiest loofah she owned. But it didn't work. Even after she'd toweled dry, she could feel him on her. It was like he'd branded a memory of his body on hers.

She had to draw a line with him and stand by it. If she didn't, she stood in real danger of losing control of her feelings, her desires…heck, her entire life! And that wouldn't do at all. She'd mapped out the life she wanted for herself, and it didn't include a high-speed surfing bum with no job and hot sex on his mind.

Girding herself to face the monstrous temptation that was Trent Hollings, she stepped out into her living room. He was out cold. As in she could pick up his hand and drop it across his stomach without disturbing him even a little.

Man, those sleeping pills of his were powerful. She scooped up the bottle and did a quick internet search of the chemicals and dosages listed on the label. Dang. One of these pills could drop ten men…and very possibly kill one man. How did his body tolerate them?

She poked around on the internet for information on insomnia. When that didn't yield anything helpful, she moved on to researching extraordinary human speed. A few articles talked about how world-class sprinters had better quick twitch reflexes than most other humans, but nothing she found could explain Trent's incredible speed.

The cab had been going well over twenty miles per hour as it pursued Trent. And he'd been pulling away from the vehicle. Which meant he was measurably one of the fastest human beings ever recorded.

Who *was* he? Or more accurately, *what* was he? If only Sunny were back from her honeymoon. Maybe she could shed some light on Trent's superhuman capabilities. After all, Sunny had been hanging out with Trent and his buddies for the past several months at the Winston compound.

Winston…hmm. That gave her an idea. She searched the internet for all of Winston's many subsidiary companies. One in particular caught her attention. Winston Computer Research, Ltd. was a small firm run by Jeff Winston personally. Trent was listed as an employee, as were all of the groomsmen in Sunny's wedding, including Chloe's new brother-in-law, Aiden McKay.

But what really made her sit up and stare was the list of other staff members. Over a dozen physicians and medical researchers were employed there. What did doctors have to do with computer research?

Using her temporary FBI access code, she poked into the bureau's records of Winston Computer Research, Ltd. and immediately ran into a firewall declaring the records she sought classified.

Was Jeff's company working with the government in some capacity? She glanced through her open door to the big man sloppily sprawled, unconscious, on her sofa. Was Trent involved with the government in some way? Was his speed the reason?

A shocking thought struck her. Or was his speed a *result* of working with the government?

She walked out into the living room and gave his foot an experimental nudge. He didn't react in any way. She turned on the television full blast. Nada. She added a radio and her stereo system to the din. Still no reaction. Frowning, she fetched a pair of pot lids from her kitchen and clanged them together directly over his head, succeeding only in making him roll over.

If she made much more noise, her neighbors were going to call the police. She turned everything off and sat down to stare at Trent sleeping away. She might as well take advantage of the opportunity to learn all she could about him.

Being careful not to disturb the contents, she searched his luggage and discovered an array of high-tech gear that looked like it would mostly be used in surveillance—

microphones, headsets, binoculars and various small electronic gadgets that looked suspiciously like bugs. But nothing in his equipment or personal possessions suggested he was any sort of secret supersoldier.

She returned to the internet to see what it could tell her about Trent's life. His family was, indeed, worth tens of millions and he was, indeed, rumored to have a substantial trust fund. His acceptance to Stanford was notable; he must have been a good high school student, and she knew him to be highly intelligent. He'd won several local surfing competitions during the first three years of an unremarkable college career. But then he apparently dropped out of school for a while. She found one reference on a surfing website that noted he'd withdrawn from a big competition due to his ongoing illness. The date placed it in the summer before his senior year of college.

An illness? What illness?

Her blood ran cold as another website gave it a name. Spinal muscular atrophy. As she read a description of the disease, she couldn't reconcile its debilitating effects with the man sleeping in her living room. He was the picture of health—and more.

She kept digging. Trent had spent the last several years traveling competing in—and winning—major surfing competitions. Clearly, his SMA had miraculously resolved itself. Did that have anything to do with all those doctors working at the "computer research" firm? An uneasy feeling nagged at her gut. She didn't see the connection, but she could feel it there, just out of sight.

His statement that he played for a living appeared to be mostly accurate, for he showed up as often in gossip columns these days as the sports pages. Clearly, he never lacked for female company. Which made his hookup with her in Denver all the weirder. He'd had his choice of all the single women at Sunny's wedding, yet he'd chosen her. As Chloe recalled, there had been plenty of good-looking women panting after him during the reception.

When he woke up, she'd have to ask him about it. If he could interrogate her about her personal life, she had no problem doing the same to him. Her internet sources exhausted and Trent still out cold, she resorted to looking at Barry's files.

Most of the records were boring and straightforward. However, after an hour or so, the very boring-ness of the files made her suspicious. As convoluted as the company's accounting methods were, there wasn't an error to be found anywhere. No company's records were this perfect.

She performed an online cross-check of a random set of receipts against the scanned originals of the invoices. Huh. The columns of pristine sales figures didn't exactly match up to the actual transactions. This must be how they were laundering money. The discrepancies weren't large, a few dollars here and there. Except it looked like money was disappearing from the accounts, not showing up in them. Laundered money would be flowing *into* legitimate accounts, not *out* of them.

A bloodhound on the scent, now, she dug deeper into the invoice files. She lost track of time and was startled to realize it had gotten dark outside when she finally looked up from her screen.

Trent had been asleep for nearly eight hours. Was something wrong with him? Should she try to wake him up? She moved into the living room to examine him. He was so still she laid an alarmed hand on his chest to see if he was still breathing.

Without warning, his hand shot up and grabbed her wrist in a movement so blindingly fast she barely saw it. She jumped, badly startled.

"What's wrong?" he bit out, sitting up so fast he nearly knocked her off her feet.

"Nothing's wrong. You've just been asleep a long time and I was checking on you."

"How long?" he rasped. His throat sounded dry.

"Eight hours."

He stared at her. "Eight? I never sleep that long."

"Well you just did."

"What have you done to me?" he demanded as he headed for the kitchen and poured himself a glass of water.

She watched, bemused, as he immediately set about broiling steak and boiling potatoes. The question wasn't what she'd done to him. It was what *he'd* done to *her*. No man had ever made her insides feel all quivery and un-certain like this.

Out of reflex, Chloe went on the offensive. "So, Trent. Tell me about the medical research you're involved with at Winston Computer Research. Doctor Gemma Jones is in charge of the program, I believe?"

The pan of boiling water slipped out of his hand and crashed to the floor, splashing scalding water all over her kitchen. And Trent jumped out of the way fast enough to avoid a single drop of it touching him. She had never, in all her life, seen another human being move that fast.

"You're not just fast. You're freakishly fast." Chloe surged to her feet. "Who are you?" she demanded.

He looked up at her grimly, his lips pressed stubbornly together.

"Or should I ask, *what* are you?"

Chapter 7

Trent knew in his gut that diverting probably wouldn't work, but still, he had to try. "I think we've been over that already. I'm a rich bum who goofs off and doesn't do anything more serious than surf big waves."

"And yet, you're on Jeff Winston's payroll. In fact, you're the man he chose to entrust my life to. Now why is that, Mr. Surfer Bum?"

Frustrated and cornered, he just stared at her, willing her to leave it alone. Of course, she didn't.

"Could it have something to do with that lightning-fast speed of yours? Tell me, Trent. Were you born with that speed? Or does this have something to do with your miracle cure of a supposedly incurable degenerative muscle disease?"

"You found out about my SMA, huh?"

"Why didn't you tell me about it?"

"It never came up in conversation. And I'm over it."

The next words out of his mouth came unbidden and he couldn't have stopped them if he tried. "Is there any history of spinal muscular atrophy in your family?"

"Not that I know of."

"Thank God." Their children would be okay. He'd still insist on genetic counseling to make sure she didn't carry a recessive gene for SMA, of course. But odds were it would have shown up at some point in her family tree if the gene was there.

She'd already circled back to the speed issue. "If you were that fast as a kid, your parents or coaches would have pushed you into sports. You'd be a superstar playing for the professional sports team of your choice or an Olympic track star."

In point of fact, if he used his skills to play any sport full out, he would probably rewrite the record books for it.

"That means," she continued relentlessly, "you came by this speed as an adult. Now how is that?"

He tried not to wince or give her any hint that she was on the right track, but it didn't slow her down. He mopped up the spilled water on the floor and started a new pot of potatoes.

"Then the self-avowed trust fund bum takes an actual job. And the job is with an obscure research company that, although it's supposedly a computer research firm, has a shocking number of physicians and medical researchers on staff. Why is that, do you suppose?"

He stared at her from the kitchen, doing his damnedest to hide his dismay. "You're the one on the logic roll. You tell me."

"You've had something done to you," she accused.

"Like what?" His voice might sound mild, but his guts were jumping all over the place. Most of it was panic that she'd somehow uncovered his secret, but a tiny part of him actually wanted her to figure it out. Sometimes it was damned hard having a secret like his and nobody to share it with. Sure, the gang at Winston Enterprises knew about the Code X research, but that wasn't the same as having someone personal—a friend, or confidante, or even a girlfriend—who knew how extraordinary he was.

He checked himself. *Extraordinary* might not be exactly the right word for it. *Strange. Bizarre. Weird.* All of those words applied to him and his colleagues. Each of the men and women in Code X had a different enhanced ability. Some were massively strong or could see for miles, while others could calculate complex math equations like a computer or swim like a fish. As for him—he was Fast. Capital *F*.

"I have no idea what they did to you," Chloe answered. "Maybe they dipped you in a vat of radioactive chemicals or hooked you up to machines or injected you with some bizarre cocktail of drugs. But you're definitely not normal."

He did wince then. She was right. He was not normal. But that didn't mean he could admit it to her. Mentally, he sighed. He knew what he had to do. He hated it, but sometimes the only decent defense was a good offense.

"Like you're one to talk," he retorted. "You act like a frigid virgin ninety-nine percent of the time, and then all of a sudden you turn into a totally different woman, uninhibited and unbelievably hot. Why is that, Chloe? Why are you so repressed? And where did you even learn to imagine some of the things you had me do to you in Denver? Not that I'm complaining, mind you. That was a night I'll never forget and one I'd like to duplicate. But what's the deal? You're like Jekyll and Hyde."

Yup. That distracted her. She reddened from hairline to neckline and spluttered in what looked like a combination of outrage and embarrassment. And guilt. She knew he was right. And he'd lay odds she knew the answers to his questions, too.

"C'mon, Chloe. What gives?"

"If I thought you actually gave half a darn about me, I might just tell you," she snapped. "But all you care about is yourself. Having a good time. Where the next party's going to be and how you're going to get the next chick into the sack with you."

So. It was brutal honesty time, was it? He could do that. And he was just frustrated enough to take the gloves off. "Since you seem to have knocked yourself out on the internet, researching me while I was asleep, when was the last time I showed up in a tabloid wearing a piece of blonde arm fluff?"

She frowned and didn't answer.

"I'll tell you when. Three summers ago. I gave up the partying and the women, cold turkey."

"Why?"

"Because Jeff Winston forced me to take a look at myself and my life. He asked me if I respected the man I had become, and I realized I didn't. With his help, I decided to make a change."

"How big a change?" Chloe challenged.

Damn. He should have known she'd be like a dog with a bone in its teeth and refuse to let go.

"A big change," he allowed. "I can neither confirm nor deny any of your speculation, but I will say the changes in my life have been dramatic."

"That's a word for it," she muttered.

"Okay, your turn," he announced. "Time for you to share something about yourself with me."

She squirmed uncomfortably, and he felt like a cad. He'd successfully avoided giving her any real information about his physical transformation and had now put her on the hot seat. It was a mean tactic. But what choice had she left him?

"When was the first time you ever had sex?" he challenged.

"That's damned personal," she snapped.

"Chicken to be honest with me?"

Her gaze narrowed. Yup, he'd pegged her as the type who wouldn't refuse a dare. She glared as she bit out, "High school."

"Did you like it?"

"No!" she blurted with enough vehemence to make him grin. "It was disgusting. And messy."

"So you've always been a neat freak?"

"Growing up, everything around me was so chaotic that I craved order. I'm not actually obsessive-compulsive like most people accuse me of being. I just want a modicum of calm. Structure. Predictability."

"And what made your childhood so chaotic?"

She sighed. "My parents were, in every clichéd sense of the word, hippies. They ran all over the world championing environmental causes. Sometimes they dragged me and my sister around after them. We had no steady school, let alone a steady home or steady income. We never knew where the next meal was coming from or if it would come. And yes, they were heavily into the whole free-love thing. Orgies were frequent events in my world."

Trent caught the tiny shiver of recollection that rippled through her. "And when they weren't dragging you along to orgies?" he asked.

"We got dumped with various friends and neighbors so they could protest." A note of bitterness crept into her voice. "Their causes were more important than their own children, apparently."

˙ Ouch. That had to hurt. Particularly for a child who'd obviously craved family and security the way Chloe had.

She continued, "I was more of an adult than they were. I practically raised Sunny."

Which might explain why Sunny didn't seem to have the same hang-ups about family and security that Chloe did. Sunny'd had a big sister who provided stability and unconditional love. But there'd been no one to do the same for Chloe. His heart ached for the lonely, abandoned child she'd been.

Chloe shrugged. "When they were around, I stole loose change from my folks and used it to keep Sunny and me fed. They were as likely to spend their money on weed as food."

"How did they die?" he asked soberly.

"Their boat went down in the Indian Ocean. Maybe a storm. Maybe pirates, maybe their own sheer stupidity." She shrugged as if she didn't care, but he sensed the deep pain behind her words. She blamed them for leaving her alone to raise her kid sister. And frankly, he had to agree with her. He would hug her if he didn't think she'd shatter completely at his touch. As it was, he stayed where he was and let her talk.

Chloe went on more reflectively. "When they died, Sunny and I were separated and tossed in the foster-care system."

He prompted, "And how was that?"

She shrugged. "Some of the homes were okay. A few of them were as bad as anything you've ever heard about. Mostly it meant more chaos in my life. I tried to keep in touch with Sunny as best I could. To let her know I loved her and was there for her."

He glanced around her apartment, seeing it with different eyes. The sparse neatness of it, the calm colors and quiet décor all made perfect sense now. No wonder she craved "normal" so desperately.

"Then what happened?" he asked.

"I figured out that getting an education and a decent job were my best bet to get out of the chaos. I graduated from high school with honors, picked up a few scholarships, worked a string of crappy jobs and went to night school, and eventually became a CPA. I even clawed my way through a master's degree. And here I am. Finally in control of my life. At least until that SUV in Denver and you came along."

"Don't you ever want to let go of all this order a little?"

"Like how?"

"I don't know. Throw your dirty laundry on the floor or leave dishes in the sink overnight."

She laughed a little. "I'm not that anal. I leave the house dirty now and then."

"Show me. Do something messy. Right now."

Abruptly serious, she replied, "You're in my life. That's the messiest thing I've done in a long time."

Ahh. A revealing observation. She didn't do relationships because they were too chaotic for her. "Is that why you avoid sex?" he blurted.

"Excuse me?"

"Do you avoid sex because it involves a relationship, and you can't control one of those entirely?"

"Of course not." Her words sounded scornful, but her eyes looked thunderstruck.

Predictably, she retreated to her bedroom, and he let her. He sensed he'd just stomped on a very sensitive nerve and she needed time to recover. She went to bed without ever emerging, and he spent the long hours of the night aching to comfort the lost and forlorn little girl she'd been.

Chloe was all business the next morning. She seemed to

have decided overnight that she was going to plow through the Paradeo financial data in its entirety today. She barely spoke to him all morning and well into the afternoon. He put a sandwich down beside her computer and she didn't even look up from the numbers she was totaling on a legal pad. Her concentration while working was as intense as when she made love. Turned on by the ferocity of her focus, he nonetheless backed out of her room silently to let her work.

By mid-afternoon, she was pacing the apartment muttering to herself over the legal pad. And by dinnertime, she was making sounds of frustration that bordered on primal screams. That was when he intervened.

"Time for a break, baby."

"What? Huh?"

"You need to step away from it for a little while. Clear your head."

She frowned but did as he instructed and fetched walking shoes and her purse. It was a balmy evening and felt good to get outside and stretch his legs. Her apartment was too tiny a cage for his taste.

"You're just itching to take off and run full out, aren't you?" she asked.

He looked down at her in surprise. "Actually, I am. But I won't leave your side."

"What's it like to run that fast?"

"It's like…flying. It's amazing."

"Is whatever they did to you permanent?"

He shrugged. "No comment."

"Aw, c'mon. It's obvious the doctors at Winston did something to you. Nobody runs that fast."

"Keep your voice down," he bit out.

"So it's classified, then?" she persisted.

"Yes," he snapped. "Very."

She looked entirely too thoughtful at that admission for his comfort. But what choice did he have? He couldn't let her blab about it on a crowded street for anybody to overhear. He led her into a park not far from her place and they walked briskly in silence.

Without warning, Chloe exclaimed, "I've got it!"

He jumped hard, startled—a downside of his superfast reflexes—and Chloe giggled at him. "I'm glad you find that funny," he growled. "What have you got?"

"A way to track the money at Paradeo. It's all about the money trail."

"What's all about the money trail?"

"Proving that they're laundering drug money. I've got to trace the money back to its illegal sources. The company will no doubt have covered its tracks by passing the money through a bunch of bank accounts. But instead of tracking the cash itself, I'm going to try tracking the transaction fees."

"The fees the banks charge for making a deposit or withdrawal?"

"Exactly. The amounts are negligible, but each bank will have a record of them somewhere. And because they're a standard and tiny fee, they shouldn't be protected by much or any encryption. Let's get back to my place so I can check out my theory. If I'm right, Paradeo's CEO will be in jail by the end of the week."

He grinned and lengthened his stride to match hers as she hurried along the sidewalk. Her passion for her work was obvious. He was quickly coming to the conclusion that she was, by nature, a passionate person. Her obsession with bloodless and emotionless order couldn't possibly be her default state of existence. But how to convince her of that? Maybe he should just engineer unbridled sexual encounters with her until she admitted she enjoyed them.

The idea had real possibilities. He spent the rest of the walk back to her place pleasurably contemplating strategies for accomplishing just that.

Chloe stepped past Trent as he swept open her apartment door with a flourish and waved her inside. The guy did a darned credible Prince Charming imitation. She flipped on the light switch inside the door and froze in horror.

Her apartment was completely trashed. Furniture was overturned and its stuffing ripped out. All the books were pulled off the shelves, the drawers pulled out, emptied and thrown on the floor. Glass was broken everywhere and sparkled on the floor like fairy dust.

A strong arm went around her waist, yanking her back hard and spinning her out into the hall. Trent uttered a single, terse word. "Run."

Terrified, she sprinted for the elevator, but Trent yanked her into the stairwell beside the elevator instead.

"Who—" she started.

"Later," he bit out.

"Why—"

"Hush."

She focused on the steps flying beneath her feet as Trent dragged her at a breakneck pace down the stairs. Who would destroy her place like that? What had the intruder been looking for? A sense of having been violated began to creep up her spine. It invaded her stomach and she was nauseous by the time they burst out of the stairwell and into the building's lobby.

Trent screeched to a halt. "Walk now," he ordered under his breath. "Try to look normal. Don't draw attention to yourself."

She stared at him in shock. "What?"

"Smile. Look like nothing's wrong. We have to get out of here without anyone noticing anything out of the ordinary about us." He punctuated his order by smiling and nodding at her.

Eyes huge with fright, she flashed him a grimace that she prayed passed for a smile. His grip on her arm was painfully tight, but she didn't complain. She nodded at a neighbor and prayed she looked sort of normal, and then they stepped out into the street.

She expected Trent to take off running, but he didn't. He strolled a few blocks to a hotel with a taxi stand and slipped the bell captain some cash to hail a cab. She piled into the vehicle numbly. What had just happened? She felt violated and off balance. Visions of her entire life grotesquely torn apart swam through her brain. She felt... naked.

Trent bit out a destination and leaned back, wrapping an arm around her shoulders and dragging her close to his side. He seemed to understand the depth of her distress and offered silent comfort. His body was big and strong and solid against hers, and she leaned against him gratefully. As the immediate crisis passed, she began to shake. Tears welled up in her eyes.

"Not yet, baby," Trent muttered. "Hold it together a little longer."

He sounded awfully tense for a man who'd made a safe getaway. What was wrong now? She sniffed and did her best to be strong as fear gripped her once more. If Trent was wired, something was definitely wrong.

And then she noticed him glancing out the back window of the cab. She did the same and saw only a tangle of vehicles. "What's up?"

"We've got a tail," he replied.

"Which car?"

"The big silver SUV about five cars back."

She picked it out without much trouble. Uh-oh. That thing could hold six or eight bad guys, easy.

Trent murmured, "We're going to have to jump out and make a run for it."

She watched in dismay as he shoved a twenty-dollar bill through the slot in the Plexiglas divider between them and the driver. He told the guy, "We're going to get out fast when we get to our destination. This should cover the fare. Keep the change."

The cabbie grinned at the giant tip and nodded.

"Ready?" Trent asked tersely.

"What happens next?" she asked querulously.

"We're going to head for the most crowded place we can find and try to lose whoever follows us. If we get separated for some reason, meet me at the Millennium Health Club on Stockton Street. Engage a private workout room in the name of Chip Jones if I haven't done so already."

"Who's that?"

"I made the name up. But it's an average name. It won't raise an alarm if someone goes in there looking for us."

She nodded, but she had no intention of getting separated from him. The idea of being alone and pursued by whoever'd destroyed her home and maybe killed Barry made her want to throw up.

The rippling glass walls of the Moscone Center—a massive convention facility—came into sight ahead and Trent reached for his door handle. "Here we go. As soon as the cab stops at the next stoplight, we'll go."

The traffic came to a halt and Trent threw open the door. Staying low, he ducked out of the cab and pulled her out with him. The door slammed shut and he took off, weaving in and out across several lanes of traffic in a half-crouch. She raced to keep up as he dodged between cars.

She stumbled up onto the sidewalk and he jerked her upright, diving into a crowd of people streaming into the Moscone Center. "What's in here?" she panted.

"Lots of people," he replied tersely.

He threw money at a ticket window and shoved a lime green, plastic hospital-style bracelet at her. They hurried through the turnstiles and into what turned out to be a giant travel expo of some kind. Colorful booths displaying alluring destinations and hawkers shoving pamphlets at her momentarily overwhelmed Chloe's panic. But then Trent grabbed her hand and urged her to hurry.

She made the mistake of glancing back over her shoulder as he dived into the crowd. A half-dozen tough-looking men had just stepped out onto the expo floor. They huddled for a moment and then dispersed. And they looked intent on murder. She turned and raced after Trent as he walked through the crowd so quickly she had to break into a jog every few steps to keep up.

"Try to look happy," he gritted out.

Right. With thugs on their tail trying to kill them or worse. She would die if something happened to Trent. Particularly if it happened while he was trying to protect her.

Meanwhile, according to all the people shoving fliers at her, paradise awaited her in an all-inclusive package that included round-trip airfare and meals. She dodged tiki hut overhangs and bikini-clad models and concentrated on keeping up with Trent. He twisted and turned, ducking between booths and racing down the long rows, seeking the thickest crowds he could find. Chloe could discern no pattern to his movements, which she supposed was the point.

All of a sudden, they popped out of the crush of honeymooners and retirees. A sign pointing to the restrooms loomed before them. Trent swerved abruptly, though, and jumped through a pair of double doors marked Employees Only.

She followed fast and emerged into an enormous kitchen. Trent had already taken off running and she gathered herself to give chase. He was probably slowing down to give her a chance to keep up with him, but his idea of slow was a run-for-your-life sprint for her. In moments, she was gasping for air and her legs burned like fire.

Trent dived left between stainless-steel worktables, and she charged after him as he accelerated away from her yet again. He shocked her by bursting through another set of doors that led back out onto the expo floor. She'd assumed they were going to sneak out some back exit and try to lose their pursuers that way. But instead, he'd circled back toward them! What was he thinking?

Of course, maybe that was the point, too. Do the unexpected and throw the bad guys off their track. Regardless, she was grateful he'd at least slowed to a walk and was winding through garish exhibits once more.

The entrance they'd come in through was drawing near and she was starting to breathe a mental sigh of relief when a voice called out of the crowd without warning, "Trent? Trent Hollings? How the hell are you, dude?"

A deeply tanned guy wearing baggy swim trunks covered in neon palm trees materialized out of the crowd in front of them. "Man, I haven't seen you since the North Shore. Where'd you disappear to, old man? You comin' back to the beach or what? The waves are bitchin'. Big surge rolling into Malibu tomorrow night."

Trent skidded to an annoyed halt, glancing over his shoulder quickly. Chloe did the same, and her blood ran cold. She spotted two thugs closing in from directly behind them, and if she wasn't mistaken, that was another one off to their left talking urgently into a cell phone. Not good.

"Go," Trent grunted at her.

"But—"

"Go!"

Horrified, she watched as the surfer dude snagged Trent's arm and shouted into a portable microphone that one of surfing's great champions was here and for everyone to give a big hand to Trent Hollings.

Trent threw her one last grim look and jerked his chin toward the exit as a crowd of surfing fans swallowed him up. All of a sudden, she was alone. No matter that thousands of people pressed in on her, jostling her.

She looked back frantically and couldn't see any of their pursuers. But that didn't mean they weren't there. She walked toward the exit, panic nipping at her heels, her steps getting faster and faster until she finally broke into a run. To heck with blending in. She raced for the door as fast as her tired legs would carry her. Faces flashed past in a kaleidoscope of irritation and frowns as she bounced off bodies heedlessly in her flight.

All of a sudden, she burst outside. The relative calm of the street startled her. She dived into the traffic, ignoring the horns that blared at her. She frantically flagged down a cab heading the opposite direction and leaped into it, shouting at the driver, "Go, go!"

Startled, the cabbie hit the gas.

Crouching low in her seat, she watched her pursuers pile into the silver SUV from before. Where had it been loitering? As the convention center retreated in the rearview window, the SUV was still struggling to make an illegal U-turn to pursue her.

"Turn here," she ordered the driver. He screeched around the corner, getting into the spirit of the thing. "Turn again," she called.

They wove across downtown San Francisco for another

dozen blocks before she finally said, "Okay. I think we lost them. Take me to the Millennium Health Club, please."

"The one on Stockton?" he asked.

"That's the one."

"What's the hurry?"

"My ex-husband has a private eye stalking me, and it's making me nuts."

"I hear you. My ex is a crazy bitch…."

She tuned out the guy's diatribe about his family troubles and lawyers demanding alimony he didn't think he should have to pay. She was still breathing hard. Trent had really run her around back there. Thank goodness he'd had the foresight to set up a meeting place if they got separated.

They had to quit splitting up, though. She hated being alone like this, so exposed. Had she always been this vulnerable and just not realized it?

She ran her credit card through the cab's card reader and typed in a generous tip for the driver. As she hopped out of the cab, he called through the window, "You need me to stick around for a minute? Make sure you get inside without that guy spotting you?"

She smiled in gratitude at the driver's kindness. "Thanks. But I'll be fine, now."

The Millennium Health Club was housed in a newly refurbished high-rise that was all brushed nickel, frosted glass and high-tech gadgetry. A male model depicted on an electronic billboard spoke up as she walked past. "Hi, Chloe! How about a fizzy break from your day?"

She swerved away, startled. How did that thing know her name? It must use some sort of credit card or I.D. sensor as people walked past it. Still, it was creepy. She stepped into a glass elevator that turned out to have no buttons in it. Great. How did this thing work?

"Where can I take you?" a honey-smooth woman's voice purred.

"Millennium Health Club."

"Right away," the elevator intoned. The doors slid shut and she shot up a clear tube into the innards of the building. She was duly disgorged on the sixth floor with an admonition by the elevator to have a great workout. Wow. Double creepy.

A blessedly human girl with a perky voice and entirely too perky body welcomed her at the front counter.

"I'm here to meet Chip Jones," Chloe said. "Is he here, yet?" She highly doubted Trent had managed to peel away from that crowd of surfing fans and somehow beat her here, but she had to ask.

"Let me check." Perky girl scanned a flat-screen monitor quickly. "I'm sorry. He hasn't arrived, yet."

"Then I guess I'd like to rent a private workout room or whatever it's called. He should be joining me shortly."

"Are you a member here, ma'am?"

Crud. Now what was she supposed to do. "Uhh, no. I'm not. But Chip is."

"No problem. I'll just use Mr. Jones's member number. After you try our facilities, perhaps you'd like to consider joining. I'm sure Mr. Jones will give you a recommendation, and I'd be happy to go over our member services with you. Our facilities are soundproof, and use one-way glass to the outside. They're completely private...."

Chloe pasted on a fake smile and mumbled something incoherent as the girl finished her canned spiel, passed her a plastic key card and pointed down a hallway to her right. This place looked like an office, not a gym. She stepped into the designated workout room and stared at the array of weights, mats, mirrors and machines before her. A dozen people could work out in here and never get in each other's way!

While she waited for Trent, she strolled around the private room, examining the various computerized machines and trying to figure out what a few of them did. Bored, she swung a personal television around on its arm to face her. Idly, she stepped onto a treadmill and strolled along to the drone of an all-news channel.

She heard the door open quietly behind her. Thank God. Trent was finally here. She turned to smile a greeting at him…and screamed as four strange men burst into the room and charged her. She dived under the treadmill's hand rail and behind a stand of assorted dumbbells. Picking one up, she heaved it at the men, shouting for all she was worth for help. But the blasted soundproof walls undoubtedly had completely contained her cries for help. One man went left and another went right. She kicked and scratched and bit as they grabbed her, but she didn't stand a chance against them all. They bodily picked her up to subdue her.

Cautiously, one of the men released his grip on her and fetched several large towels from the heated rack in the corner. He wrapped her tightly in the thick terry cloth, effectively immobilizing her. He stuffed a wadded washcloth in her mouth for good measure. Furious and frightened, she glared at her captors.

"Here's how this is going to work," the towel guy said in a Hispanic accent. "We're going to walk out of here like we're all friends and everything's fine. If you so much as look at anyone wrong, we're going to kill the girl at the front counter and anyone else who tries to help you."

Horror roared through Chloe. These guys were going to murder innocent people on her account? That was *awful!*

"You got it?" he demanded.

She nodded, deflated. No way would she be responsible for someone else's life being taken. It was bad enough dealing with her guilt over Barry's death. And he'd taken those files entirely on his own with no prompting from her.

"Okay. We're gonna let you go now. But my guys all have guns. See?"

The other thugs obliged by flashing pistol butts under their sports coats.

"Not a peep out of you. Not one hint there's a problem," her captor warned as he reached for the door handle.

Chloe walked as slowly as she could out of the room and down the hall, hoping against hope that Trent would step out of the elevator and rescue her. But he didn't. The phalanx of armed men hustled her into the elevator.

"Going down?" the elevator asked pleasantly.

"Lobby," the leader growled.

"Si, señor. Tiene una tarde agradable."

How on earth did the elevator know to tell this guy to have a nice evening in Spanish? She risked commenting, "Even the elevator knows who you are. And so does my bodyguard. He's going to track you down and take you out if you don't turn me loose right now."

Her threat only made her captors laugh. So much for intimidating these guys. Her throat went dry when she contemplated what these men might do to her. All of a sudden, she understood all too well Don Fratello's comment that some things were worse than death. When they reached the street she was going to put up a fight whether these jerks liked it or not. But when they stepped out of the elevator, they didn't head for the lobby. Rather, they turned left and hustled her deeper into the building.

They used a dim, concrete stairwell that stood in marked contrast to the shiny modernity of the rest of the building, and she stumbled down the steps as someone shoved her from behind.

"I'm going to fall and break my neck if you push me again like that," she snapped over her shoulder. "And obviously your boss doesn't want me dead, or you guys would have shot me already."

Her captors scowled and one of them made a rude comment in Spanish about what a bitch she was. She didn't bother acknowledging that she'd understood him. The steel security door at the base of the stairs opened to reveal a grim underground parking garage. Nobody would hear her scream down here.

They had to pass between a row of parked cars, and she faked a stumble against a door handle in hopes of snagging her shirt and leaving behind a thread or something to indicate she'd been here.

Her plan worked a little better than she'd anticipated. Her entire shirt snagged on the handle, and when one of the thugs gave her a hard shove, the hem tore with a loud ripping sound. She steadied herself against the car's window, leaving what she hoped was a perfect handprint on the glass.

The leader, who was in front, growled something about hurrying up, and the guy behind her shoved her again. He could really quit doing that. It was starting to get on her nerves.

No surprise, she got shoved into the middle seat of the silver SUV and men squeezed in on either side of her. She was surprised, however, that they didn't seem to care if she saw where they were taking her. That couldn't be good. They must expect to kill her after they extracted whatever they wanted from her.

But when the SUV pulled to a stop in front of its destination a short time later, she abruptly understood. They'd taken her to Paradeo's offices. And that was when she broke out in a cold sweat.

Chapter 8

Trent was on the verge of doing violence to his surfing buddy by the time he managed to peel himself away from the crowd the guy'd blithely gathered around to hem him in.

He searched frantically for their pursuers. Were they lurking nearby waiting for him to make a move? But there was no sign of a single one of them. That answered that. This wasn't about him and Code X at all. As he'd suspected, these guys were purely after Chloe. He swore violently and his terror climbed another notch.

If she'd done as he ordered and run for it, she'd had enough of a head start that she should have been able to get outside and fade into the crowd. Maybe grab a taxi or duck into a store and hide. *If. Should. Maybe.* Dangerous words to hang a person's life and limb on. Particularly a woman he cared about greatly.

He didn't panic often, but he panicked now. She had to

be okay. The idea of her injured or worse made his chest feel like someone had blown a massive hole through it.

She was no doubt cooling her jets at the Millennium Club, bored out of her mind and wondering where the heck he was. He would join her there, and she was going to laugh her head off at him for worrying that she couldn't take care of herself.

He headed outside of the Moscone Center to hail a cab, and while he waved at taxis he dialed her cell phone. It rang three times, clicked, and then cut off. That was weird. Not only had she not answered, but it hadn't kicked over to voice mail. The hole in his chest expanded until it choked off his breathing. He dialed again, praying fervently that her wireless network had just dropped the call. This time, he got a message that the number he'd dialed was not available.

Swearing in a continuous stream, he jumped into a cab and bit out the address of the Millennium Club and urged the driver to hurry. He'd run, but the streets were still crowded, and, at all costs, he couldn't give away Code X by letting the public see his mad speed. Of course, telling a cabbie to hurry was like giving a crack addict a shot of adrenaline. The taxi ride turned into a death-defying stunt derby…and he didn't care in the least.

He raced past all the cool electronics in the health club's lobby and fretted impatiently as the elevator whisked him up to the sixth floor. Racing to the health club's front counter, he asked urgently, "Has Chip Jones arrived yet?"

The receptionist smiled. "A woman showed up asking for him a while ago. And then those other men came and she left with them."

It was all Trent could do not to dive across the counter and grab her shirt. "What men?" he demanded sharply.

The receptionist recoiled in alarm. "There were four of

them. In suits. She walked out with them like she knew them."

"Let me see the room she was in," he ordered. He was scaring the receptionist to death, but he had no time to play nice. Something was terribly wrong.

"Of course," the girl stammered. She led him down a hallway to a closed door and leaned down to swipe the master key card hanging from a lanyard around her neck. He barged past the girl into the room.

Empty. Damn! The hum of the treadmill running was the next thing he noticed. And then the dumbbells scattered on the floor. As if they'd been tossed willy-nilly. Crap. Had Chloe been trying to defend herself?

A pile of towels in the middle of the floor and a lone washcloth made no sense. He took another look at the washcloth. It was wadded up and looked damp. Like it had been shoved in someone's mouth. He swore more violently.

At least there wasn't any sign of blood. If her captors merely planned to kill her, here would have been as good a place as any. These rooms were soundproof, and had he not come along demanding entrance, this room would have been left undisturbed for the rest of the evening. This was a very discreet club.

Apparently, someone wanted to talk to her before she died. And that meant he had a window of time to find and rescue her. Possibly a very small one, but it was better than nothing.

"Did they head down in the elevator?" he asked the girl tersely.

"Uhh, yes. I guess so."

"How long ago?"

"A few minutes."

"Is there a parking garage under this building?" he yelled as he sprinted for the exit.

"Yes!" the girl called at his back.

No time for the elevator. He slammed his shoulder against the stairwell door and burst through it, taking entire flights of stairs in a single leap as he practically flew downward. There was a chance…a tiny one…that her captors hadn't left the building yet with her. He tore through the lobby and burst out onto the side street where the parking garage had to empty out. He looked left and right.

A silver SUV was stopped at a red light about a block away. Was it the same one that had been following them earlier? He glanced at the black maw of the parking garage. Should he head inside to check for Chloe or should he follow that SUV on the chance that it was her?

He had only a millisecond to make the decision. His gut said not to lose that SUV. He stretched his legs out into a full run, devouring the pavement with each stride as he tore toward the vehicle. The light turned green and it pulled away from him. No way was he losing it! He pushed for even greater speed, determined to catch the vehicle. It turned a corner, and he swerved after it, dodging pedestrians and ignoring the occasional squawk as he shoved past someone.

Despite his incredible speed, the SUV gradually pulled away from him. He began to suck for air, and then to gasp for it. His thighs burned like acid, and muscles pushed beyond all human limits finally began to cramp and fail.

Devastated, he searched the avenue ahead and could find no sign of his quarry. He glanced around to get his bearings. Maybe the police could pick up the trail. And that meant a quick call to Winston Ops to pull some strings with the San Francisco Police Department—

It dawned on him abruptly that he was only a block from the Paradeo office. And it was in the same direction the SUV had been heading. What were the odds?

He took off running again, this time at something resembling a normal human speed. It was the best his exhausted body could manage. And frankly, he was starting
to feel a little light-headed. He must have burned through
a gazillion calories with that mad dash across the city.

Five minutes brought him to the Paradeo building. *Be
inside, Chloe. Be alive, baby.*

He burst into the lobby, which was deserted after business hours, and reluctantly admitted to himself that he'd
better take the elevator up to Paradeo's floor. It was im-
mensely frustrating to have his body give out on him like
this. Normally, anything he could imagine, he could do.
Did comic book heroes ever feel like this?

The elevator dinged open and he eased out to one side.
The space yawning before him was dim. Only every tenth
overhead light or so was lit. A cubicle farm stretched away
from him, still and deserted. If thugs from Paradeo had
grabbed her, they would take her someplace private and
quiet to question her. His mind shied away from imagining them doing anything else to gentle Chloe.

He slid along the wall, hugging the shadows and gliding
silently across the carpeted floors. All of Paradeo's offices
were on this floor. They would probably take her someplace tucked away in the back of the building. Skirting
the open cubicles, he passed a pair of conference rooms.
A hallway narrowed before him and he slowed, easing toward the first closed door.

She had to be here. She just had to.

Chloe had seriously expected to wind up in some
dank, dark alley or deserted warehouse, not in a perfectly normal-looking, antiseptic office in the very place
where she worked. She'd assumed they would want to torture her to death in peace. Where no one would hear her

screams. She tested the duct tape that secured her wrists to the arms of an office chair. Not a chance she was getting loose anytime soon.

She nodded in unsurprised recognition when Miguel Herrera stepped into the office. Of course he was behind her kidnapping.

"Miss Jordan."

She stared up at him. *What did he want from her?* The unspoken question vibrated angrily between them. What was so important that he had to treat her like a criminal and kidnap her?

"My employers want their money back, Miss Jordan."

Money? What on earth? "What money?" she blurted.

"The money you stole from Paradeo."

"That I—" *Was this guy crazy?* She was looking for funny business Paradeo's executives were pulling, not doing the stealing herself! "I haven't stolen anything from Paradeo!"

Herrera sighed and perched on a corner of the desk in front of her. "We can do this the easy way or the hard way. But make no mistake. Before you walk out of here, you're going to tell me how you did it, where those funds are now, and how to transfer them back to Paradeo."

"Well, Mr. Herrera, that's going to be a bit difficult since I didn't take any money, I'm not hiding it anywhere and I cannot return what I didn't take."

"Make no mistake, Miss Jordan. I will not hesitate to turn the boys loose on you."

She glanced over involuntarily at the four big men, standing silent, eerily eager, in front of the window. A shudder passed through her. Never had any of her forensic accounting professors mentioned that she might find herself duct-taped to a chair with a roomful of thugs flexing their fists in anticipation of pummeling her senseless...

or much worse. This was a nightmare. Fear for her life coursed through her anew. The idea of suffering the kind of pain these men could so easily inflict on her turned her insides to water.

Trent hadn't been wrong, after all. She'd been an ignorant fool to believe she was safe from harm.

She looked Herrera directly in the eye and saw only hard determination. There would be no quarter granted from this man. The calming effect of finding herself in such a normal and familiar environment fell away as the true jeopardy of her situation sunk in.

Satisfaction gleamed in Herrera's black gaze as he loomed over her. "Talk to me, Chloe."

She closed her eyes for a moment to draw strength from within. "Mr. Herrera. I am telling you the God's honest truth. I have never taken a dime from this company."

"Hah! Do you need me to show you the records? The missing funds, a little bit here and there? And funny thing, all from accounts you have direct access to."

"How much money are we talking here?" she asked, curious in spite of her terror. Not to mention, if she kept the guy talking, it delayed the inevitable moment when he lost patience and turned the dogs loose on her.

"You tell me."

"I don't know. I didn't take it."

"How long have you been with this company?"

"What does that have to do with whether or not I took your missing money?" she blurted.

"Answer the question," he snapped. But he frowned at her, almost as if perplexed.

"Six months, give or take. How long has the money been going missing for?"

"About four months."

"If it's that recent, it should be reasonably easy to track down. It can't have gone too far," she replied reasonably.

"Where exactly has the money gone?" he repeated darkly. It didn't take a rocket scientist to see that this man didn't have a whole lot of patience, and what little he had was wearing out fast. She eyed his meaty fists warily. This was really going to hurt. How was it she could go so damned fast from feeling so strong and in control of her life to feeling so weak and completely *not* in control? Was the order she imposed on her world that thin a veneer?

Understanding exploded across her brain. She'd been deluding herself all along. Life had always been this scary and insecure, and she'd been lying to herself to think otherwise. She could no more force the world to conform to her needs any more than she could Trent. She felt adrift, at sea without a life jacket, totally at the mercy of the currents she floated upon. She had, without question, never been this terrified in her entire life.

Her voice shook as she stated with all the sincerity she could muster, "I have no idea where your funds have gone. You can ask me the question a hundred different ways, but my answer is always going to be the same... because it's the truth. I didn't take any money and I don't know where it is."

He leaned down close to her, his breath hot in her ear. Her skin crawled and she leaned away as far as her bound wrists would allow, but it wasn't far enough.

He followed, murmuring, "You think you can steal from me and mine and we won't make you pay? You think if we show weakness to our enemies they won't turn on us like rabid dogs? You think I'm gonna let you walk out of here alive? That I won't make you suffer until you scream and beg and sing like a canary?"

She shook her head, too terrified to make a sound. She'd

seen the news. Heard the stories of the atrocities the drug cartels inflicted on their victims.

"Imagine the worst thing you've ever heard my kind doing to an enemy. Multiply it by a hundred. A thousand. Before I'm done with you, little girl, you're going to be a front-page news headline that shocks the world. You have no idea how much suffering a human being is capable of. But I'm going to show you every last bit of pain your body can stand. And I'll just be getting warmed up."

Her knees were already shaking, but the rest of her joined in as adrenaline surged through her veins, screaming at her to run for her life.

"You'll try to scream, but I'll cut your tongue out. You'll gabble like an idiot and choke on your own blood. And no one will hear you. I'll skin you slowly, peeling the flesh back in strips to expose nerves you never knew you had. You think having your flesh burned to a blackened crisp and your muscles charred to the bone sounds bad? Oh, you'll find out for yourself. And I'll just be getting warmed up."

She was going to be sick. Her body twitched in horrified anticipation of the things he was describing, and her nerves tingled from head to foot, demanding that she run away. Begging for it. Sobbing for it.

"Did you know that the only pain in the human body you're not able to pass out to escape comes from the kidney? I'm going to stick needles in yours. The pain will be so exquisite you'll beg me to kill you. And there will be *no* escape. It'll go on and on and on until you literally go mad from the agony of it. And I'll still just be getting warmed up."

Oh, God. Kill her now.

"There are twenty-six bones in the human foot, twenty-eight if you count the sesamoids at the base of the big toe. I'm going to break them one by one with a hammer. You'll be a cripple for the rest of your life. And if you still haven't told me what I want to know, I'll do the same to all twenty-seven bones in your hands. One by one. I'll smash them into useless pulp. You'll be unable to perform even the simplest tasks for yourself. And then I'll start on your teeth. I'll break them in your jaw, and then I'll pull out the pieces one by one. And all the while, you won't be able to scream. Won't be able to escape it. And then we'll move on to the real torture. Things so horrible that even contemplating them will make you scream."

She realized that tears were running down her cheeks and that rattling sound was her teeth chattering in abject terror.

"Do you need a small demonstration, little girl?"

She shook her head violently in the negative, her throat muscles so convulsed with fear she couldn't make a sound.

He leaned down to murmur in her ear, "If you scream, maybe I won't kill you so soon. You hear me? Scream for me, little girl." Without warning, he ripped the duct tape off her left wrist.

And she did scream. At the tops of her lungs. Every hair on her forearm had been pulled out by the roots, and tiny droplets of blood sprinkled across her flesh where the tape had forcibly torn off the outer layers of her skin. Her wrist went from ghost white to brilliant scarlet as she stared at it. Her arm felt as if she'd laid it on a stove burner and left it there long after her body shouted at her to yank it away. Tears ran down her cheeks as the stinging intensified and insulted nerves roared their displeasure.

She became aware of a whimpering noise and realized with a start that it was coming from her. Herrera reached for her other wrist. Sounds began to pour out of her mouth in a steady, pleading stream. "Nonononoonoooo…"

* * *

Trent jolted into motion as Chloe screamed. Someone might as well have stabbed him, so sharp and visceral was his reaction to the thought that someone was hurting her. A powerful need to kill flowed through him, giving his limbs lightness and speed, his mind a hyperawareness, that even he'd never experienced before.

At least he knew she was in the building and approximately where she was. Given that there was no one out here acting as a lookout, he had to assume that all four of the guys who'd been chasing them in the Moscone Center were in that room with her. He couldn't take them all at once. He needed to draw one or two of them out and pick them off. He looked around and spotted a wood-backed chair behind a receptionist's station. Perfect.

Ducking down behind the station, he intentionally banged the hard, wooden slats into the desk. He didn't have long to wait. A door opened, and the sound of Chloe moaning floated out to him. Trent's gut tightened. *Hang on just a few more minutes, baby.*

After a cautious check of the darkened hallway, two men surged out like fire ants protecting their mound. He ducked to avoid being spotted. The good news was neither man had pulled a gun. Yet. He waited until they'd split up and were moving away from him before he pounced. The first man was a piece of cake. He never saw Trent coming. A fast chop to the back of the guy's head and the big man went down like a tree.

Small problem: trees don't fall silently. The second man whirled, and all chance of surprising him was blown. Trent took a wary step backward. Glanced over his shoulder as if contemplating fleeing. It was too easy. The thug bought Trent's head fake and attacked on the assumption that

Trent was scared stiff and planning to run rather than stand and fight.

Time seemed to slow. Trent watched the thug's mouth open on a silent yell, his legs pump in exaggerated slow motion, his hands come up like glacial claws creeping forward toward his prey.

Trent ducked under the slowly arcing fist with casual ease, his own hands coming up to pummel the guy's vulnerable face. The problem with thick, muscular targets was that body blows had little immediate effect on them. For a fast takedown, he went for the bridge of the nose. The temples. Eyes.

In a flurry that even his gaze struggled to follow, he slammed his fists into the attacker's face over and over. Streams of blood flew through the air like tiny red rainbows, and the thug's torso arced away from the assault. The guy fell heavily to his knees, then toppled over, face first.

The office door opened and three more men poured out into the hall. Not good. Trent might be fast, but his build ran to the lean side and he was of average strength. Three huge guys landing on him would effectively immobilize him no matter how fast he was when loose.

He turned to run, hopefully to lead the men away from Chloe and give her time to escape. The men scrambled to give chase, and as they careened around the corner, the one in the lead stumbled. He threw his arms wide, knocking his buddies off balance, as well. Flailing like a human windmill, the first guy staggered into the second, knocking him into the third.

Looking over his shoulder, Trent watched in shock and relief as all three men went down in a pile. He spun on a dime, raced back toward the swearing and shouting pile of men and hurdled them all. He skidded into the room Chloe was in, and she looked up in panic.

Her tear-stained face was terrified and he bit out, "Let's go."

"I can't," she wailed, clawing at her ankles.

He saw the problem immediately. Her left ankle was taped to the leg of a chair. It appeared she'd already torn loose the tape securing her right ankle. He snatched up a letter opener off the desk and stabbed at the half-torn tape. She grabbed the loose end, gritted her teeth, and gave it a yank. A sharp gasp and she was free.

He pulled her out of the chair and half out of the room in one mighty heave. She stumbled and righted herself as they raced out into the hall. Shouting and swearing erupted behind them as her kidnappers struggled to untangle themselves and gain their feet.

"Run for your life," Trent grunted.

Chloe took off in an impressive sprint, and he kept pace beside her using his excess capacity for speed to yank chairs into the aisle behind them and even to pull over a tall filing cabinet to block their pursuers' path. As it crashed to the floor, a cloud of flying paper filled the air behind them.

"Call the elevator," he ordered as he paused just shy of the elevator bank to pull out more furniture and create a pile of obstacles for the thugs to navigate. Pounding footsteps announced that they had untangled themselves and were giving chase.

An elevator dinged behind him as three big, angry shadows burst into view. "It's here. Hurry, Trent," Chloe called urgently.

He dived around the corner and into the elevator with her. She was already mashing the Close Door button frantically. Would those doors *never* move?

The footsteps grew louder. Finally, ever so slowly, the elevator doors began to slide shut. A shout went up in Spanish. Trent swore in a steady stream under his breath. They weren't going to make it out of here before the bad guys caught up with them. He braced himself to jump. If it came to it, he would throw himself out there and buy Chloe the few extra seconds she needed to escape. Whatever had been planned for her would end up being perpetrated upon him, but so be it. She *had* to get out of here alive.

The guy who'd stumbled before slid around the corner, and promptly slipped on a manila file folder. Yet again, his feet went out from under him and he neatly leg-tackled the thug who was just barreling around the corner behind him. Both men went down.

The doors were halfway closed now. Through the gap, Trent recognized with shock the face of the clumsy man. Miguel Herrera. The Chief of Security for Paradeo. He was personally involved with this kidnapping? What was so important about Chloe that a man in his position would risk himself directly? Why not pass the dirty work to low-level henchmen who would take the fall for it if they got caught?

The doors shut with a quiet whoosh, and the car started downward. Trent's taut body relaxed a tiny bit. Chloe took a sobbing breath and turned into him, burying her face against his chest. He wrapped his arms around her, panting. "Catch your breath, baby. We're not home free, yet."

She lifted her head to stare at him in dismay.

"We'll get a little head start because of the elevator, but you can be sure your kidnappers are running down the stairs this very moment. And they may have someone in the lobby waiting for us."

"What are we going to do?" she gasped.

"When the doors open, we're going to run out like a pair

of charging bulls. Plow right through anyone who stands in your way. When we hit the street, turn right. There's a big hotel about a block down and it'll have a taxi stand with plenty of cabs."

"Where do we meet if we get split up?" she asked fearfully.

"Go to the nearest police station and call Jeff Winston. But we're not going to get split up this time."

"Promise?" she asked as the elevator lurched gently to a stop.

"Promise." And then the doors slid open and it was time to run again.

No one was waiting for them in the lobby and they burst out onto the street together. Chloe veered right and ran beside him with the choppy strides of panic. She collapsed into a cab with him, hyperventilating. He gave an address to the driver and turned to her in concern.

"Did they hurt you? Are you all right?"

She nodded, unable to speak. Whether she was nodding to having been hurt or to being all right, he couldn't tell. He turned his attention to her more immediate crisis. "Hold your breath and try to count to three before you exhale. You need to build up more carbon dioxide in your blood to settle down your breathing."

It took her several tries to follow his instructions, but gradually, her breathing deepened from shallow pants to something vaguely resembling normal.

The cab approached the block where she lived and Chloe was recovered enough to ask in alarm, "What are you doing? We can't go back to my place. Herrera knows where I live!"

"We're not going to your place. We're going to mine."

She stared at him, uncomprehending.

Trent explained, "When I first got to San Francisco,

I rented a room in a bed-and-breakfast across the street from your apartment so I could watch you, remember? I've still got that room. And frankly, I doubt Herrera and his pals will look for us so close to your place. We need somewhere to crash until we can form a plan and get some backup into town."

She nodded wearily. He knew the feeling. The crash after a big adrenaline surge was a killer. And the idea of Chloe being hurt or killed by her kidnappers had definitely been a major adrenaline event for him. He was going to need to sleep fairly soon. But there was no way he could go down for the count until Chloe was safe.

He instructed the cabbie to let them out around the block from Chloe's apartment. No sense making her visible to Herrera's men if they were staking out her place. He ushered her out of the cab, tucking her protectively under his arm as he led her into the B&B. They went directly up to his room, and as he hung out the Do Not Disturb sign and double locked the door, she moved over to the window.

"Wow. You do have a great view of my place from here," she commented dryly.

He moved over beside her and gazed down into her living room. "Yup. I saw every move you made."

"That is so creepy."

He put his hands on her shoulders and tugged her back to lean against him. "I assure you, it was only for your safety. I would never have invaded your privacy like that unless it was a matter of life and death."

She sighed, a gentle nudge of her ribs against his chest. "I guess we've established that Herrera and his goons are out to do me serious harm?"

"I'd say so. How are your wrists and ankles? Your skin looks pretty mad."

She looked down at the red stripes across her fair skin.

They looked like scraped knees and burned like them, too. "I need to wash them and get some antibiotic cream on them."

But neither moved to treat her wounds. Instead, they stood still, leaning against one another, silently savoring the fact that they were alive. There would be time enough in a minute or two to get back to business. Right now, they needed to acknowledge that they'd survived a near miss with death.

"Thank you for coming after me," she murmured.

His hands tightened on her shoulders. Like it or not, this was no longer entirely business for him. Somewhere along the way his feelings for her had become personal. "I couldn't live with myself if anything happened to you, Chloe. I...care...about you." *A lot.*

More than he'd realized until he'd watched her running from her pursuers in the Moscone Center and he'd been helpless to protect her. More than he'd realized until he'd heard her scream and it had felt like his own heart getting ripped out. More than he'd realized until he'd been prepared to leap through the gap of those closing elevator doors and sacrifice himself to save her.

She shuddered in his arms, clearly in need of some serious reassurance. He drew her gently to the bed and sat down, leaning back against the headboard. She curled against him like a frightened baby animal seeking comfort. His heart literally ached for her.

"Tell me everything that happened," he said quietly.

She described the chase through the Moscone Center, her terror when Herrera's men grabbed her, the shock of realizing they were taking her to Paradeo's offices. He was not surprised by the sequence of events. But then she told him how Herrera demanded to know where Paradeo's money was.

"He thought *you* were embezzling from Paradeo?" Trent exclaimed.

"Weird, huh? Here I am trying to find how their money's being laundered and what's wrong with their books, and so are they."

"There's a thief inside the company," he breathed. Shock vibrated through him.

"But who would dare steal money from a dangerous drug cartel?" Chloe asked.

"Someone who doesn't know who they are, I suppose."

"Or someone who doesn't care," she added.

He froze beneath her. "Are you telling me you think some rival of the cartel behind Paradeo is making a move on it?" Good God. If there was about to be a drug turf war, he had to get Chloe out of town and far, far away from the violence about to erupt.

"I don't know if another cartel's moving in or not. But I know where to find the answer."

"Barry's files."

"Exactly. I need to finish my analysis. And fast. At least I know now why I kept finding anomalies I couldn't explain. I was looking at two financial crimes and not one. If we can find this thief before Herrera does, maybe the FBI can turn him or her into an informant. The thief could testify against Paradeo in return for some sort of plea deal or immunity from prosecution."

He didn't particularly relish the idea of racing Paradeo's violent security chief to identify whoever was brave enough to steal from a vicious and efficient drug cartel.

Chloe was speaking again, "But I need a computer and internet access to do it."

"Done." He leaned over and picked up the telephone. In a moment, the owner of the B and B had agreed to send up a laptop computer and a laser printer within the hour.

"How did you get the owner of this place to do that for you?" she asked curiously as he hung up.

He frowned. "Why wouldn't he?"

"Because you could steal the thing and rip him off."

He shrugged. "I told him to buy me new equipment and charge it to my room bill."

"You charged a *computer* to room service?" she asked incredulously.

"Better living through trust-fund-assisted convenience," he remarked dryly.

"No kidding," she grumbled.

"Is my having money a deal breaker?" he asked soberly.

"Depends on the deal," she replied cautiously.

Now there was the sixty-four-thousand-dollar question. What deal, indeed?

Chapter 9

She slept that night, and Trent slept the next day while she worked. Herrera had mentioned small amounts taken from many accounts she had access to, and now that Chloe knew what she was looking for, the work went more quickly. She was able to pick out the trail of the laundering from the trail of the embezzling more easily. If someone was taking money from Paradeo, the thief was doing it very well and leaving practically no traces.

As the day wore on, though, something else began to dawn on Chloe. Herrera hadn't been wrong. The missing funds all came from accounts she was directly responsible for. If she didn't know better, she'd say *she* was the thief. Alarm started to vibrate low in her gut, gradually growing in volume and intensity as the afternoon wore on.

Who else in the company had access to the same accounts she did? She poked around but no one else had exactly the same financial footprint as hers. Paradeo was a highly compartmentalized company, and no matter how hard she searched, she couldn't find anyone else with access to all of her accounts. Not good. Not good at all.

Trent woke and immediately asked that food be brought up to them, but she ignored the plate he set down beside her. Eventually, he actually took her by the shoulders and turned her away from the computer. "You need to take a break, Chloe. Eat. Drink some water. Stretch your muscles a little."

Now that he mentioned it, her stomach was growling and her throat did feel rough with thirst. It didn't help that her alarm had grown into panic clawing at the back of her throat.

"Any progress?" he asked as she picked up a sandwich and commenced eating.

She winced. "I'm on the trail of something. I've identified a number of tampered-with transactions, and now that I've seen what accounts the thief is targeting and how he or she is disguising the thefts, I should be able to spot more fishy transactions quickly. Once I do that, I ought to be able to give you an idea of how much money has been stolen."

"When will you know who's taking it?"

"Honestly, it looks like I'm the only person with access to all the accounts the thief stole from. I may have a hard time finding someone else to add to the suspect list." She blurted, "I've got to solve this or else I could be in serious trouble."

"Are you being framed?"

She stared at him in dismay. It was entirely possible. But who could be setting her up?

"You'll figure it out," he said encouragingly. But his smile didn't reach his beautiful gaze. Instead, worried crinkles formed at the corners of his eyes. Worry that she shared in spades.

"The FBI will crack this thing as soon as they look at the files I sent them, and they'll come looking for me. They could knock on that door at any minute," she admitted, giving voice to her greatest fear. Urgency tightened her entire body into a tense mass of jangling nerves. She was running out of time. "I didn't sign up for this, Trent. I'm just a lousy accountant doing what I was hired to do, darn it."

He snorted. "Just an accountant a major drug cartel is trying to kill. Clearly, you're more important and more knowledgeable than you seem to think."

"I don't see how. Anyone with the most rudimentary forensic accounting training could do what I'm doing."

Trent tilted his head, his gaze surprised. "Seriously?"

She nodded, depressed.

"Why did the FBI hire you specifically, then, to investigate this firm? Do you have some particular expertise in this kind of company?"

"Honestly, I have no idea why Don hired me. I'm fresh out of school with nary a job credit on my résumé. I was shocked—and wildly grateful—when he hired me. Maybe no one else was available to move to San Francisco on short notice."

Trent stared at her thoughtfully. "That is weird. You've been out of school, what, seven months? So this Fratello guy hired you straight out of college, as in—ink still wet on your diploma?"

She stared, shocked. How did Trent know so much about her? Horror flowed through her in a muddy torrent. "Did you have Novak do that deep background check on me, after all?"

"No. Your graduation date showed up in the superficial

search Winston Ops performed on you right after the attack in Denver. We were purely trying to figure out why someone might want to kill you. We weren't trying to pry into your life."

Oh, God. She didn't want to know what else they'd uncovered on her. Thank God she didn't have an arrest record or any outstanding parking tickets! "You sure do your research, don't you?" she managed to grumble past the dry tuna lodged in her throat.

A sudden, sharp longing swept over her. If only she were more to Trent than just a job. What was wrong with her that no one was interested in her as a woman? Clearly she was unlovable and managing somehow to convey that to every eligible bachelor she encountered.

"It's my past, isn't it?" she blurted.

Trent stared blankly. "Excuse me?"

"That's why no one ever loves me. There's some key lesson I failed to learn, some deep flaw in me because I got so little love in my childhood, isn't there?"

He was in front of her almost too fast to see. "What are you talking about?" he demanded.

"I'm talking about me. About why nobody loves me."

"From what I saw in Denver, your sister seems devoted to you. I'm sure you've got plenty of friends who care deeply about you."

She was shocked to feel tears well up in her eyes. Good grief, what was that all about? She was never this weepy and hormonal. "I'm sorry. I guess the stress of all this is getting to me. Just ignore me."

"No, I'm not going to ignore you. Talk to me."

She wasn't used to anyone getting this pushy with her and her impulse was to run and hide. But she knew how fast Trent was. No way would she reach the bathroom and get the door locked before he blocked it open. Instead, she sighed and retreated into her work. "I've got to get back to the computer."

"After we talk about this. What makes you think you're unlovable?"

"Oh, I don't know. The empirical evidence of no one actually loving me, ever?"

"Are we talking about you wanting a long-term relationship with a man?" he asked carefully. Lord, he sounded like he thought her head was going to start spinning around in circles or demons would leap out of the top of her skull.

"I'm not crazy," she announced.

"Okay. I believe you. You're not crazy," he replied evenly. He didn't look like he was lying, thank goodness.

"Is it too much to ask for me to find someone who likes me a little?"

"I like you a lot," he answered promptly.

"I'm talking about romantically. As in a real relationship," she snapped.

His answer came more slowly this time. "So am I."

She stared at him, stunned. "You are not."

"Yes, I am." He looked as stunned as she must look.

"Are not."

"Are you seriously going to argue with me for telling you that I like you and am interested in pursuing a romantic relationship with you?" he demanded.

"I guess I am. Particularly since I don't think you mean it."

He snorted. "And there's your answer. If you kick to the curb every guy who shows the slightest interest in you, you're going to have a hell of time getting this relationship you say you crave."

He might as well have slugged her in the stomach. Was he right? Was she pushing away anyone who cared about her? So. She was broken, after all. It *was* all her fault.

Deflated, she pulled the laptop in front of her once more. But the focus had gone out of her search. She struggled to see patterns that had been crystal-clear to her a half hour ago. It was no use. She was done for the night.

"I'm going to bed," she announced.

He sighed. "Okay. I'll stand watch until you wake up."

She glared at him. "You need more than that three-hour nap you took earlier."

"Actually, I don't. That'll keep me going a couple days."

"It's my life. I'd say it's my call."

He raised a skeptical eyebrow. "And how are you planning to force me to sleep if I don't want to?"

She pursed her lips. She might not be able to force him, but she'd bet she could tire him out enough to go to sleep on his own. As soon as she thought about sex with him, a craving to be with him, to turn herself over to him, to lose herself in him ripped through her. Was she really that needy? Or was she just more messed up in the head than she'd ever realized? She desperately wanted to escape the fear and uncertainty swirling through her and just to feel safe for once.

It dawned on her belatedly that Trent was watching her far too alertly. He looked like a tiger on the hunt. A sudden need to be his prey, to let him stalk her and conquer her made her knees weak. Did she dare?

It was crazy to even contemplate. He would break her heart as sure as she was standing here. He'd love her and leave her without a backward glance.

So, then, the trick was not to get emotionally involved with him, her inner sex kitten argued persuasively. Right. No problem. Enjoy the sex. Embrace the raw pleasure. Escape reality for a little while. And then walk away, herself. She could do that, right?

Doubt wriggled like a parasite deep within her mind,

a disgusting, dark secret she shied away from in horror. She was not her parents' child, was not ruled by passion or her emotions! She *could* walk away from Trent, darn it. She was in control of her world. Of her emotions. Of her life. No man would ever change that!

A desperate need to prove it to herself, to shut up that niggling doubt eating at her soul, buried itself in her gut. She had to do this. To show herself once and for all that no man would ever have the power to destroy her or her world.

Recklessness coursed through her, and she rode the wave, rising to her feet and walking resolutely to the mini-refrigerator. It was stocked with tiny bottles of various liquors just like a regular hotel.

Trent pushed away from the doorway where he leaned, watching her cautiously. His eyes blazed, but his body was taut with something more akin to caution. Tonight was her night. No matter what they did together, no matter what he made her feel, she would remain in total control of herself. She was the master of her mind, her body, and her traitorous feelings. He had no power over her, and she was going to prove it to both of them.

She pulled out a mini-bottle of whiskey, but Trent was there in a flash, lifting it out of her hands. He announced grimly, "If you have to drink in order to make love with me, you're going to give me a serious complex."

She stared at him in open challenge. "Don't you think you can handle me when I cut loose? What's the matter? Afraid of where I'll go with you?"

His gaze burned as hot and turbulent as the core of a volcano. "I'm not afraid of you, Chloe. I can take anything you can dish out and more."

She seriously doubted that.

But his stark observation cut through all the noise in her head, leaving behind only her determination to do this. Once and for all, she was going to purge her fear of the chaos a man would bring to her life. But could she be that brave, sexy woman that she'd been in Denver on her own? Only one way to find out.

"What do you want, Chloe?" His voice was a silken sword, so smooth and sharp it cut her to ribbons before she even realized it had touched her skin.

"I want to show you—" she corrected herself "—to show me, once and for all, that I am in control of my life."

He tilted his head, staring at her quizzically, obviously turning over her declaration in his mind. "No one's always in control, Chloe."

She shook her head in denial, and he continued, ignoring her.

"Life is messy whether you like it or not. Take you, for example. You need love in the worst way, but you're hell-bent on holding anyone who might give you that love at arm's length. You're so afraid of being hurt or rejected that you can't let yourself take the chance."

Hah! Doing this was the riskiest thing she'd ever contemplated! "You're wrong—" she started. But he swooped in and pressed his fingers against her lips, forcibly stilling them.

"Don't play with fire, unless you're willing to get burned, Chloe."

"What is that supposed to mean?" she snapped.

"It means that if you plan to seduce me in some sort of twisted power play, you'd better be prepared to lose."

She heard the words, but no meaning registered on her mind. She clung to her denial, to her determination, to her desperate need to restore order in her universe. She might not be able to stop bad guys from chasing her or trying to kill her or framing her for a crime she didn't commit. She might not be able to keep them from trashing her apartment and slashing her clothes. But by golly, she could control this. Trent would not get inside her heart or her head. She could have the wildest, hottest sex with him either of them could imagine, and it would...not...touch...her.

Her gaze narrowed. "Give it your best shot, Trent Hollings."

Chapter 10

Trent took a mental deep breath. This was it. Either he broke through all her barriers tonight, or odds were she'd never let anyone get close enough to try it again. Ever. And she was too vital and sensual a woman to let that happen to. She might not know it, yet, but she needed him to break down her walls. Hell, she needed him to smash them to dust.

He considered her for a moment longer. *And he knew exactly how he was going to do it.*

He reached slowly for the hem of her shirt and stripped it over her head. Her bra was cut low and had flirty lace trim. As his gaze dropped to the view, her hands started up to cover her cleavage.

"Ah, ah, ah," he murmured warningly.

Her hands snapped back down abruptly, fisting at her sides. Resolution darkened her gaze. What the hell was he doing? He was no fan of sex as a form of emotional combat. Of course, she was in for a surprise when he changed up the rules of engagement for this particular battle. She thought it was a fight against him, but actually, it would be pitched war against herself.

He reached for the zipper of her jeans, and she sucked in a sharp breath. He pushed the denim down over the sweet curve of her hip, and he saw the source of her chagrin. A smile split his face. "She still wears thongs, does she? I'm so proud of you."

Chloe scowled back at him. "It was small and easy to grab fast."

Right. As if he bought that lame excuse. But if she still needed her excuses to explain away her entirely normal and natural urge to feel a little sexy, he would let her have them…for now.

He lifted each of her feet in turn to ease her shoes and socks off. Since he offered her no help with her balance, she ended up having to grab his shoulder to steady herself while he massaged the arches of her slender feet. One of his goals tonight was to get her to touch him of her own free will—often and intimately, in fact.

Her right foot still cradled in his palm, he looked up at her. "If anything we do tonight gets too intense for you, let me know, okay?"

As he expected, her gaze narrowed at the implied challenge.

"I mean it, Chloe. This isn't a competition. You don't have to do anything you don't want to. Got it?"

She murmured something vaguely resembling agreement. He supposed it was the best he could hope for in her current frame of mind. She looked girded for Spanish Inquisition-style torture. Oh, he planned to torture her, all right, but not like that.

He reached around behind her, his gaze locked with

hers, to unhook her bra. For just a moment, he thought he glimpsed a flash of fear. His hands froze and he waited until it faded from her gaze. He murmured, "Where's that brave, adventurous girl from Denver who ravished me within an inch of my life? I know she can do this."

Gratitude flickered in her azure eyes as her expression steadied and gained confidence. She nodded and whispered, "Continue."

Her bra fell away from her beautiful, delicate breasts. He could look at them forever and never get tired of their elegant shape or the way they fit in his hands.

"Do you have to stare at me like that?" she asked a little grumpily. "It makes me self-conscious."

He laughed darkly. "I'm going to look all I want. And then I'm going to do all I want with you."

A fine shiver rippled across her skin. "I could really use a couple of shots of whiskey."

He replied sympathetically, "Looking for a little liquid courage? You might lose a few inhibitions in a glass of whiskey, baby, but you'd still be the same person. Most people don't change as much as they'd like to think when they drink, and they certainly don't get cooler. They just get dumber."

She smiled in spite of herself.

"Remember what I told you in Denver? Don't overthink it."

"Right. Don't overthink." She reached for his belt buckle, and he let her. In a hurry to get it over with, was she? Well, she was in for a surprise, then. He planned to take most of the night doing this.

As she reached hurriedly for his shirt buttons, he captured her hands. "Easy, baby. Slow down. Relax and enjoy the moment."

She rolled her eyes. "I can't say as I've ever found sex relaxing."

He responded, "Note to self—end the night with slow, lazy sex. To show Chloe how relaxing sex can be."

Her eyes widened and darkened. She liked that idea, did she? He grinned to himself. Good to know. There was hope for her, yet. "So, Chloe. We still have a whole lot on your list of fantasies from Denver to get through. Any preferences?"

Her cheeks bloomed scarlet. "You choose," she mumbled.

Perfect. What he had planned for tonight wasn't on her list at all. "Into the bathroom, then," he announced matter-of-factly.

She frowned, obviously going through her list and trying to figure out which one involved the restroom. Her frown deepened and alarm bloomed in her gaze. Excellent. She was already outside her comfort zone.

"Why the bathroom?" she asked cautiously.

He merely took her hand and led her, half-resisting, into the small, subway-tiled space. Without releasing her hand, he plugged the big, claw-foot tub and turned on the hot water full blast. He poured in a generous dollop of bubble bath the B and B had thoughtfully provided, and the room filled with the smell of raspberries and vanilla. Mounds of fluffy bubbles formed, and the water steamed. Tendrils of fine hair curled around Chloe's face, framing it sweetly. He added just enough cold water to make the bath bearable.

"In you go," he announced cheerfully as he rolled up his sleeves.

"Are you coming in with me?" she asked doubtfully.

"Nope. I'm designated back scrubber, tonight. Besides, I'd take up the whole tub. This treat's just for you." He perched a hip on the edge of the tub, which put her lovely breasts at eye level for him. He drank in the view eagerly as her nipples abruptly tightened into tense little peaks. Good. He wanted her hyperaware of her body before this was all said and done. It was high time she got out of her head and acknowledged her most basic bodily urges.

He leaned over to the shelf above the sink and grabbed the big, plastic hair clip she'd put there. Reaching around behind her, which brought his mouth into entirely pleasing proximity with her chest, he twisted her hair up and off her neck, securing it with the clawed clip.

She would have stepped back, but he kept his hands behind her neck, trapping her in place. Leisurely, he took a rosy peak into his mouth, rolling his tongue around the little bud and scraping his teeth lightly across it until she exhaled on a light moan. Only then did his hands fall away from the back of her neck. She didn't step back. *Chalk up a win in the first skirmish to him.*

He gestured for her to climb into her bath, but she hesitated. He reached for her thong, using it to tug her between his knees. Hooking his thumbs under the hip straps, he whisked it off her body. She curled in on herself, embarrassed by her nakedness.

"You're so damned beautiful," he breathed. "Someday, I'll have you painted in the nude."

She stared, dismayed. "And where would you hang the resulting painting?"

"In my bedroom, of course. In a place of honor by the bed you sleep in."

Her eyes popped wide open in shock. Frankly, he was a little shocked himself to realize he was thinking in terms of years down the road with her. At least his comment had the effect of distracting her from her lack of clothing. That was, until he leaned forward and kissed her belly. An urge to plant his child within her, to watch this part of her swell with the miracle of life about knocked him off the edge of the tub. Whoa. *Not ready for kids, yet.* Hell, he didn't even know if their genetics were compatible enough to have kids. He had to give her credit. Chloe did a hell of a number on his head. Damn. Skirmish number two to her.

"Into the tub, darlin'," he directed. He held her hand as she climbed over the high edge and her leg disappeared into the bubbles.

She sank down into the steaming water by slow degrees. He'd made it as hot as he thought she could stand because she needed the tension relief badly. Eventually, she sat immersed to her neck in bubbles. He folded a towel and she leaned her head back against it.

"Close your eyes," he instructed.

"Mmm. With pleasure," she murmured.

He went out into the main room to prepare for the next part of his assault while she soaked her bones to the consistency of cooked spaghetti and her muscles to gelatin. When he was satisfied with his work, he returned to the bathroom. The mirror was fogged over, and the tropical humidity plastered his shirt to him in a matter of seconds. He solved that problem by shedding it and dumping it on the floor.

Chloe's eyes remained closed as he moved to the head of the tub and reached through the diminishing suds for her shoulders. Gently, he kneaded the slender muscles. If she'd been boneless before, she melted now. He moved around to the other end of the tub and reached into the hot water for her left leg. Starting at her knee, he massaged his way down her slim calf to her toes and back up again. He gave the same treatment to her other leg. She groaned in lazy pleasure and he reveled in the sound.

The bubbles were breaking into little white islands on

the surface of the water that afforded him glimpses of her rosy body here and there. He would never forget her in this moment, his own private sea nymph.

"I think my fingers have turned into prunes," she murmured.

He plunged his forearm into the water and pulled the drain plug out of the water. She stood up and he reached for the shower head on its flexible hose. He rinsed the remaining bubbles off her and reveled in how she looked, standing there. Quickly, so she wouldn't chill and lose the languid relaxation of her bath, he wrapped her in a fluffy bath sheet that enveloped her entire body. When she was cocooned in soft terry cloth, he scooped her up in his arms and carried her into the other room.

"Oh, Trent," she breathed.

He glanced around at the dozens of candles casting a soft glow through the space. The B and B owner's wife had even provided an armful of roses from her garden for the occasion. A dozen of the most stunning roses stood in a vase on the table. He had scattered the petals from the rest across the bed and floor in a splash of reds, pinks and whites. The heady perfume filled his nose, nearly as intoxicating as the woman in his arms.

He put her on her feet and slowly unwrapped her like his own personal gift. He smudged off the remaining moisture from her skin and released her hair from its clip. It fell in a glorious shimmer of silk across her breasts. The candlelight kissed her skin with gold. This was exactly how he wanted her painted.

He picked up his nymph and laid her down gently on the bed of roses. As he stepped back to admire the effect of her sleek limbs and pale skin against the brilliant shades of the rose petals, he revised his opinion. *This* was how he wanted her painted.

Her hands drifted up to cover her private places, and he stepped forward to capture them with his hands. Holding both of her slender wrists in one fist, he lifted her arms over her head, which had the most excellent side effect of thrusting her breasts up toward him. He leaned down to feather kisses across the tempting mounds until she arched up into his mouth of her own volition.

"Are you going to tie me up?" she whispered breathily.

He lifted his head to stare down at her. "I have a better idea. Take hold of the headboard here." He guided her fingers around two of the turned spindles. "If you let go, I'll stop whatever I'm doing. But as long as you hold on, I'll keep going."

Confusion flickered in her gaze, but she nodded her agreement readily enough. Mentally, he smiled darkly. She had no idea how that promise was going to come back to bite her. He would use her own passion against her. It would restrain her a hundred times more effectively than any rope.

He trailed his fingertips down her arms, and she wriggled as he approached her ticklish ribs. She let go of the spindles and he yanked his hands away from her. Immediately, she grabbed the headboard again. He took up where he'd left off, stroking his fingertips beneath her breasts, circling the mounds lightly. Without warning, he flicked his thumbnails across both of her nipples and she arched up sharply on a gasp of startled pleasure.

He resumed his leisurely trailing of fingertips across her skin. And so it went. He touched her lightly, interspersing the lightest of massages with occasional reminders of just how sensually charged her body was becoming. The rosy glow of the bath on her skin was replaced by a rosier glow of desire.

She sang him a veritable symphony of sighs, moans

and groans of wordless pleasure as he explored her body. In Denver, they'd been driven so hard by their desire that they'd never really slowed down for him to learn her body thoroughly. But tonight, he rectified that oversight. He found her ticklish places, the sensitive spots, the areas that made her fists flex on the spindles in frustration.

And when he finished exploring with his hands, he started all over again with his mouth. As soon as she figured out what he was about, she groaned aloud. "I can't take this, Trent. You're killing me."

He replied against her hip, "Then let go of the headboard."

Her only answer was a thick groan. He smiled against her satin flesh. Ahh, she was beginning to learn the nature of the warfare he waged against her. Time to scale the next wall: her self-consciousness.

He rose up over her and reached for her ankles. Until now, her legs had been pressed tightly together, and he'd let her have her modesty. She made a sound of protest as he pushed her knees apart far enough for him to kneel between them. But when his mouth closed over her big toe and his tongue darted between her toes, the sound of protest turned into a groan of approval. He nipped the pad of her toe and scraped his teeth across the arch of her foot until she squirmed, giggling. But, he noted with approval, she didn't let go of the headboard.

He gave the same treatment to her other foot. Her breathing became short and fast as she discovered the erogenous connection between her feet and her nether regions. He had a sneaking suspicion his nymph was going to develop a bit of a foot fetish before this night was over.

When she was panting hard, he nipped his way up to the back of her knee and laved the soft flesh there with his tongue. She twisted and turned beneath him as the sensations in other parts of her built to a fever pitch.

By the time he finished with her other knee, she started to beg. "Enough, Trent. No more. It's too much. I can't…"

And yet, she continued to grip the headboard as if her life depended on it. Granting her no quarter, he nipped and licked his way up the inside of her thigh. She was openly thrashing now, flinging her limbs wide and unintentionally giving him ready access to his ultimate target.

His mouth closed on her swollen, hot flesh and she all but came off the bed. Careful not to touch any part of her except the heaving, trembling flesh beneath his tongue, he launched a full-scale assault.

She cried out his name, and he maintained contact as she bucked and shuddered beneath him. He was far from done, however. He pressed his offensive, driving onward as she climaxed again, her entire body stretching into a taut bow.

"Trent!" she cried out, her voice begging for relief.

Oh, no. He would accept nothing less than her complete surrender. This was war. He sucked and licked and circled her flesh with tongue and lips, and when fatigue began to set into her limbs, he plunged his fingers into her tight heat.

She responded instantly, her entire body tensing for an endless, suspended moment around his invasion. He felt the mother of all orgasms rip through her, and she keened in complete and violent surrender as she literally came apart for him.

Finally taking pity on her, he lifted his head to gaze down at her. Slowly, her eyes blinked open and they were glazed with such pleasure that he doubted she knew her own name at the moment. Okay, this was definitely how he wanted her painted.

Obviously, he would have to do the painting himself. This was not a sight he ever planned to share with anyone else. Chloe was his. Her pleasure and her passion were his. Why she'd chosen him to share this intensely private part of herself with, he had no idea. But he treasured the gift beyond all else.

When she'd caught her breath and a small measure of awareness had flickered back into her eyes, he murmured, "Ready for more?"

"More?" she repeated blankly.

He smiled darkly. "The night is young, my dear."

Chloe stared up at Trent in complete disbelief. There was more than *that?* He just given her the most epic, shattering pleasure of her life. What more could there be? Her fingers ached from squeezing the headboard so tightly and her palms were all but cramping from the pleasure he'd given her. But as long as she was hanging on to the wooden spindles, she was in control. She had the power to call this thing off any time she wanted. Except she emphatically didn't want.

"More, huh?" she murmured. He'd already put his hands—and mouth—on every square inch of her. No man had ever touched most of the places he'd been tonight. But it was Trent. In spite of his infuriating secrets, in spite of his casual disdain for the order she craved, and especially in spite of his ease with floating in and out of relationships, she trusted him.

He might talk about her sleeping in his bed years from now, but she knew it for the insincere pickup line it was. She knew from her research that he had never allowed any woman to pin him down. She *knew* he would leave her someday, probably sooner rather than later. But none of it mattered. Not with the echoes of orgasm after orgasm reverberating through her entire being. He made her feel like a whole woman. He made her feel...loved.

Shock rocked her to her core. Wait a minute. Tonight was about her staying in control. Of proving that no man could touch her or her world. She could impose order on her life no matter what he made her feel!

But then his fingers started to move, dancing upon her most sensitive flesh, caressing and flicking at the epicenter of her earlier detonations. Her body responded eagerly, the terrible, exhilarating tension already building deep within her once more. He knew her better than she knew herself. He stroked and teased, drawing reactions from her flesh she didn't even know she was capable of.

Her eyes drifted closed, and the lure of pure, molten pleasure called to her. She felt the volcano deep in her soul and strained toward it, sinking ever deeper toward her most primal core. When she reached the heart of this indescribable feeling, she would gladly hurl herself into it, no matter that she would be incinerated by it, entirely consumed by it.

A warning hummed vaguely in her mind. She was losing herself in the pleasures of the flesh. Her mind was being subsumed by lust. But, ahh, it felt *so* good. Still, as incredible as what he'd done to her had felt, she had to let go of that headboard.

His finger slipped into her slick heat and muscles she didn't know she had gripped the invader tightly as it slid in and out with delicious languor. The volcano surged forward, threatening to blow at any second. *Must. Fight. This. Pleasure.*

A second finger joined the first, stretching her and filling her. And then Trent started doing the most clever things, rubbing and teasing internal nerves that roared to life and pushed the volcano right to the very edge.

She would let go of the headboard any second. Just a tiny bit more of this insane pleasure. Just a tiny bit more…

When the explosion came, it made everything that had come before pale by comparison. It erupted from the depths of her soul, ripping away the very walls of her existence, throwing the scattered bits of her to the heavens in a spectacular display that lit the night. It went on and on until she didn't know if it would ever end. And somewhere along the way, she ceased to care. She gave herself over to it, emptying her entire soul into this endless moment.

It was as if her whole life had built up inside an enclosed magma chamber, deep, deep underground. The stored up pressure had been unbelievable, beyond even her wildest imagining. Only when it completely blew like this did she finally understand the enormity of what she'd been carrying around inside her.

It all came out at once. Tears of pain and joy, longing and loneliness. Ambition and fear, dreams and loss, laughter and rage. Everything she was and wanted to be poured out of her in that apocalyptic release.

And finally, when it was all too much for her, the orgasm completely overwhelmed her and everything went black.

She blinked her eyes open—it could have been a second or an hour later—and Trent was there, his body warm and solid against the length of hers. He was propped up on one elbow, staring down at her. Even now, he gave her no quarter, his gaze capturing hers in no uncertain terms, allowing her no place to hide.

"How do you feel?" he asked.

She considered. "Empty."

His brows drew together in the beginning of a frown and she elaborated hastily. "Good empty."

"How so?"

"It's as if I've been carrying around this massive burden of…stuff…inside me for so long I didn't even know it was there. And now it's just…gone. I feel light. Empty."

"Got it."

"Do you?" she murmured. "I'm not sure I do."

He merely smiled down at her and offered no explanation. "You're still hanging on to the headboard."

She blinked up at him, not making the connection to his meaning for a moment. "Oh." She started to let go and was surprised to discover that her fingers were cramped into tight fists.

He reached up with his free hand to still her hands. "I wasn't suggesting that you had to let go. I was merely making an observation. Do you want to let go? Or will you let me fill that empty place within you?"

She gazed up at him, not quite understanding his meaning. Comprehension hovered just beyond the edges of her consciousness. That, and a compulsion to hang on to that headboard just a little bit longer and find out what he meant.

Her mouth curved into a slow smile. "I'm game if you are."

Trent laughed quietly. "Ahh, sweet Chloe. You are a brave woman. Let's see what we can do about that empty feeling."

He shifted until he rested between her thighs, supporting his weight on his elbows. He didn't move. He just lay there, staring down at her. And the strangest thing happened. Her body started, unbelievably, to respond to him once more. He didn't touch her, or kiss her, or even move against her. He just continued to stare deep into her eyes. It was if he'd stripped her soul bare and gained some sort of magical power over it. All she had to do was remember the pleasure and lust he'd brought forth from her and it was all right there. The building heat, the jangling need, the wild rush toward completion.

"How do you do that?" she whispered, amazed.

He merely smiled, his gaze enigmatic. And when she thought she was going to explode yet again, he thankfully shifted. Male flesh pressed impatiently against her and she shifted to bring their bodies into perfect alignment. And then he filled her, indeed. The stretching sensation was extraordinary, her ultrasensitized flesh weeping its pleasure.

She unraveled in a matter of seconds, crying out against his shoulder as he began to move within her. The exquisite pleasure went on forever, growing in force and power as he surged toward some unseen destination, drawing her with him. She hung on to him with legs and internal muscles wrapping herself around him body and soul and clinging tightly as he took her to the stars one last time.

As her now hoarse cries built in the back of her throat and the volcano gathered itself to explode one last time and incinerate them both, he froze, tensing against her.

"Do you surrender?" he demanded, his voice rasping with desperate control tenuously maintained.

"What?" she gasped.

"Do you surrender? Unconditionally and completely?"

"Yes," she groaned as he slammed into her, shoving her over the edge and into the heart of the beast. They burned up together, hanging on to one another for dear life as the volcano took them both. Her flesh and his fused into one. They had no beginning and end, just this moment of scorching perfection they'd made together.

Consumed and reborn in the same instant, she lost herself in Trent's eyes and found herself staring back.

They must have stayed that way for a long time, but she'd lost all sense of time passing in the wonder and discovery of it all. She'd had no idea...never guessed...but then, what they'd just done went a lot deeper than mere sex....

And then it dawned on her. *This* was what love felt like.

She let go of the headboard then and wrapped her arms around the man who'd finally had the courage to break down her stupid walls and silly misconceptions to truly and unconditionally love her. And then she cried.

Trent was deeply alarmed when Chloe burst into tears without warning. He'd meant to knock her off her rocker with great sex, not make her sob uncontrollably in his arms. He rolled onto his side and gathered her against him, completely flummoxed.

"What's wrong, baby?" he murmured into her tangled hair.

"Nothing," she mumbled wetly against his chest.

Huh? Women were the damnedest creatures, sometimes. He tried again. "What's upsetting you? Tell me."

"I'm happy." She hiccuped in punctuation to her declaration.

"You want me to fix that? Am I supposed to return you to your previously unhappy state?" God, he was confused.

"No, silly." A sobbing breath. "I'm crying because I'm happy and there's nothing to fix."

"Oh." Well okay, then. He'd never made a woman cry because the sex had been so great. He relaxed and drew her across his chest as he rolled over onto his back. She was warm and silken and boneless against him, just the way a satisfied woman should be. He was feeling pretty damned boneless himself, at the moment.

They relaxed like that for a long time. Long enough that he was just on the verge of slipping into unconsciousness before it dawned on him that he was actually falling asleep without drug assistance. Go figure. Epic sex apparently cured his insomnia. He drifted once more, reveling in the feeling of going to sleep with this gradual, natural ease.

Chloe murmured against his chest, "I know you'll leave me someday, and I'll probably be too mad to tell you then, but thank you for this night."

His eyes popped open and his body abruptly tensed. So much for sleep. "What do you mean I'll leave you?" he demanded.

She rolled off his chest and laid on her back, staring up at the ceiling. She answered matter-of-factly, "It's not like you've ever made any secret of your lifestyle. You're a playboy. You travel the world, and lord knows, the beaches you hang out on are full of girls all too eager to jump in the sack with you. Why would a hot guy like you settle down with a girl like me?"

He pushed up onto an elbow to glare down at her.

She continued, not looking over at him, "Denver was a casual hookup for you, and had someone not tried to kill me, we would never have seen each other again."

He'd been plotting ways to see her again before he'd ever climbed out of her bed that night in Denver. "Yes, we damned well would have seen each other again," he burst out.

That made her look his way. She recoiled, and he realized he was probably glaring daggers at her. Tough. She was really pissing him off. "News flash, Chloe. What we shared tonight was damned special. Once-in-a-lifetime stuff."

"Well sure, it was the best sex I've ever had, but I'm not like you. I don't have a ton of experience."

"That was not sex! That was making love, dammit!" He probably shouldn't be yelling at her like this, but he couldn't seem to help it. She seriously thought tonight had been some casual thing for him?

"I bared my soul to you, Chloe, and I thought you'd done the same to me." He exploded out of bed, too agitated to lie still another instant. He moved around the room fast, grabbing up bits and pieces of his clothes. He yanked a fresh shirt out of his bag and pulled it over his head.

Chloe was sitting up in bed, the sheets pooled around her waist, a red rose petal clinging to her left breast just over her heart. "How in the *hell* do you do that, Trent?"

He whirled to glare at her. "Do what?" he snapped.

"You move so fast my eye can barely follow the movement. No human being moves like that. What have they *done* to you?"

"They," he spit out the word angrily, "saved my life. They gave me stem cell transplants that restored my muscle tone and then some. Jeff Winston saved my life, but to do so he had to turn me into a superhero. Have you got a problem with that?"

She just stared, apparently struck speechless.

On that note, he stormed out the door and slammed it shut with an entirely satisfying reverberation of angry sound behind him.

The streets were dark and deserted. He stretched his legs into a ground-devouring run and flew into the darkness, losing himself in the night.

Chloe stood in the shadows of the room, peering around the edge of the curtains, using the rough cloth to hide her nakedness. And as Trent raced away from her at the speed of sound, a tear slid down her cheek.

What *had* they done to him? Jeff Winston and his doctors had turned Trent into some kind of freak. The inability to sleep, the incredible metabolism, and the speed. God, his speed. She'd never seen a human being even begin to move that fast as he'd raced away from her. Was it a fair trade-off? Life in return for being a circus sideshow? He'd been gone so quickly she'd barely had time to register what she'd seen.

And now she was alone. Again. Just like always, anyone she'd dared to love had run screaming from her at the first available opportunity. This time, it hadn't been enough for the guy to run away at normal speed. No, this one had run from her at superhuman speed.

She slid down the wall beside the window and curled into a little ball, hugging her knees and burying her forehead on them. This time, she wasn't going to recover. Trent had shown her just how magnificent love could truly be, and she had no illusions that she would ever find another man who could take her to the places he had. How could she ever settle for anything less?

No doubt about it. He'd ruined her heart. For good.

Chapter 11

Sometime during the night, Chloe dragged herself back to bed and pulled the covers up over her head. When she awoke, the morning outside was foggy and gray, totally appropriate to her mood. There was no sign of Trent having returned to the room during the night.

Heart heavy, she sat down at her computer and listlessly opened up Barry's files to poke at them. The entire list of files took a while to load, and she stared at the blinking cursor, blank-eyed. Idly, she wondered how he'd managed to get access to all of these files. She didn't come close to having the security codes to get half of these files....

And then it hit her. How *did* Barry get access to all of these files? God, it had been right in front of her all along! Paradeo was a highly compartmentalized company. *No one* had access to all the financial information sitting before her. Barry had to have broken into multiple servers to retrieve all this information. But how?

He had managed to get passwords and access codes for at least three different systems within the company. And if he could break into the servers, he could also break into every single account on those servers. Was *he* the thief?

Immediate guilt for suspecting a dead man swamped her and she pushed away the notion. But her brain kept circling back to it. There truly was no one else at Paradeo who could be the thief. Even the Chief Financial Officer had to have other members of his staff open locked servers for him when he wanted access to them. It was the one cardinal rule of the firm. Nobody could touch everything.

Except Barry had managed to do it. Had he been working alone? Or did he have a cadre of accomplices? Lord knew, enough money was missing for several people to live comfortably on it for a long time. Her calculations showed the missing funds to be on the order of twenty million dollars.

This must be why he'd been murdered. But then Chloe frowned. Why had Miguel Herrera accused her of stealing money from Paradeo if the big bosses had already identified and eliminated the thief? They must think she was one of the accomplices.

She picked up her cell phone and called Don Fratello but was passed immediately to his voice mail. "Don. It's Chloe. I've found something big at Paradeo. This isn't just a money laundering problem at all. It's an embezzlement case, too. Barry Lind—that bookkeeper who was murdered a few days ago—was stealing money from Paradeo. Lots of it. We're talking millions. I think he had help, though. If you look at his bank records, I'll bet he's been passing money to one or more people who've been helping him. The FBI should be able to track down his accomplices easily. Call me when you get this message."

Satisfied, she hung up the phone. A quick double-check

of the last time money had been skimmed off an account made her jaw drop. Yesterday. Even after Barry had been brutally murdered, his accomplice had continued to steal. She had to give the unknown person credit for having nerves of steel. No way would she have kept taking money right from under Paradeo's nose if she thought violent drug lords were on to her.

There was still plenty of work left to be done tracking down where Paradeo's money came from in the first place. The original money laundering case was still open. But it was time to hand that over to the FBI. It would take their resources and access to privileged banking information to track the transactions back to their various sources. She had all the starting points identified, though, and it would be an easy matter for the FBI to finish the investigation.

Which left her at loose ends with not much work to do. And that meant she had plenty of time to ponder her own mess of a life. She glanced at the time. Nearly 8:00 a.m. Where was Trent? Was he ever coming back?

Reluctantly, she picked up her cell phone again and stared at it doubtfully. She was too chicken to dial him directly after last night. He'd been so furious when she confronted him with the truth. But there was no way he would stick around for the long haul with any woman. It was written all over him. She'd merely read the obvious signs and called him on it.

He was right about one thing, though. She had a knack for pushing men away from her. Slowly, she dialed the Winston Ops phone number.

"Winston Ops. Good morning, Miss Jordan. What can we do for you today? Did you lose Trent again?"

It was the duty controller, Novak. She steadied her voice as it started to tremble. "Actually, I did. He left last night a little after midnight and he's still not back." Her voice dropped to a tearful half whisper in spite of her best efforts as she confessed, "I don't know what to do."

"Trent ordered up a full security team for you sometime last night. I can look up the time if you want. It was before I came on duty. At any rate, they're inbound to you now. Should be there in a couple of hours."

Oh, God. He'd washed his hands of her. Trent was handing her off to a bunch of strangers rather than look out for her himself. The pain of his departure cut right through her, eviscerating her soul. Her legs collapsed and she found herself sitting on the floor again, leaning against the bed this time.

"Just a moment, ma'am. I'll get Jeff." God, did Novak have to sound so sympathetic? She was so pathetic.

Jeff Winston's voice came on the line in a matter of seconds. "What's wrong, Chloe?"

It was the last straw. He was so gentle and sounded so concerned. She slapped her hand over her phone's microphone jack as a sob escaped her.

"Chloe? Where's Trent? What's going on? Are you okay?"

She dragged in another sobbing breath and then steadied herself. She had to get through this conversation. "I don't know where he's gone, Jeff. He left last night." She added reluctantly, "We had a fight."

Give the man credit for not asking what about. Instead he went for the safer but obvious question. "Are you in a secure location right now?"

"Yes. I'm in the hotel room Trent was using to do surveillance on my apartment."

"Stay there. We've got a team on a jet. They'll land in San Francisco in about—" he paused while somebody no doubt supplied the answer "—two hours. They should be with you by noon."

"I don't need your team," she replied wearily. "I solved my case a little while ago. Or at least the part that was going to get me killed."

"Really?" Jeff responded with interest.

She filled him in briefly, ending with an assurance that the FBI could take the case from here. The big dogs at Paradeo should find out the identity of Barry's actual accomplice(s) just in time to call their dogs off her before they went to jail themselves for money laundering. "And so," she concluded, "I'm pretty much off the hook."

Jeff made a noncommittal noise. "Still, I'd like to keep a few guys on you until the FBI's investigation is wrapped up and Paradeo's senior managers are behind bars. Just for your sister's peace of mind."

"Why does everyone keeping using Sunny to guilt me into cooperating? She's a grown woman and can take care of herself. She's got Aiden and doesn't need me anymore."

Jeff answered quietly, "We always need our family, Chloe. Sunny loves you wholeheartedly. She'd die if something happened to you. Why do you think she asked me to keep an eye on you in the first place? She was worried about your new line of work getting you into trouble. Frankly, if not for her concern, you could be dead right now."

"How's that?" Chloe asked, startled.

"It was because of her that I asked Trent to keep an eye on you at the wedding. Had he not been there to knock you out of the way, that SUV would have hit you."

Oh. My. God. *Trent had spent the night with her in Denver because he was under orders to?* He hadn't even wanted to hook up with her in the first place! Her humiliation was complete. And then she'd asked him to do all those things… God, what he must think of her. Poor, desperate, spinster sister of his buddy's hot bride. Where was a rock for her to crawl under and never come out?

She mumbled something incoherent and all but hung up on Jeff Winston. No way was she sticking around for another team of his guys to come and take pity on her. Gee whiz, maybe they'd give her a group orgy if she acted pitiful enough. Her skin crawled at what Jeff and his men must think of her.

Oh, God…what must Trent think of her? Not that it had kept him from having sex with her whenever he wanted it, of course. In the wake of her gut-squirming humiliation, anger took root, growing like Jack's beanstalk until it reached the sky and beyond. How dare he?

Literally shaking with fury, she punched out Winston Ops's phone number once more.

"Hi, Chloe, what can I do for you, now?" Novak asked cautiously.

"Where's Trent?"

"Excuse me?"

"I know you can track his cell phone. You did it before. Where is he right this second?" Her tone of voice brooked no refusal.

"Uhh, just a sec," Novak muttered. "He's in Malibu. Or rather, off the coast of Malibu."

"Like in the ocean?" Chloe asked in surprise.

"Yes. I'd imagine he's surfing. He's pretty good at it, you know. World champ two years ago—"

She hung up on Trent's accomplishments. Whatever. World champion surfer, world champion jerk. Same diff. Eyes narrowed, she considered how to find him and give him a serious piece of her mind. Her car. It was in the parking garage underneath her building across the street. She had to get to it without Herrera or whoever might be staking out her place spotting her.

She headed downstairs to ask the owner of the B and B for a favor. If the guy could buy Trent a laptop, he could certainly fetch her car for her. Sure enough, the fellow was more than happy to trot across the street and get her car for his best customer's girlfriend.

Right. Girlfriend. What the guy didn't know wouldn't hurt him. In a matter of minutes, she was seated behind the wheel of her car and on her way south out of San Francisco. It was nearly four hundred miles to Malibu, but traffic was moving fast on I-5 and she made outstanding time, killing the trip in a little under seven furious hours. Plenty of time to work up a really good head of steam.

It was late afternoon when she parked beside the Malibu Pier. If Trent was surfing, he was no doubt doing so at Surfrider Beach, just north of the pier. It was a blustery day and she secured her hair in a ponytail as it whipped in her face. She grabbed a sweater out of the trunk of her car and held it tightly around her body as she slogged out onto the sand.

The ocean roared its anger and only a few people sat or strolled on the beach. The water was dotted with dozens of surfers, however. And she could see why. The waves were easily twenty feet tall, and the occasional big wave topped thirty feet. These waves were not for amateurs. But then Trent was a world champion.

A half-dozen Jet Skis hauled wet-suit-clad surfers up and down the swells, depositing them just beyond where the breakers started. Which one of the neon-colored specks was Trent? Shielding her eyes from the wind and flying sand, she squinted out to sea.

"Looking for someone?" A grizzled beachcomber startled her by asking from right beside her.

"Uhh, yes. Trent Hollings."

"Hollings. Let's see. Big, good-looking guy. Dark hair.

Light eyes. Prefers a left-hand curl...big wave rider. Uses a long board. That the one?"

"Yes. That's him." She didn't know what kind of waves Trent preferred or what kind of board he used, but the physical description certainly fit.

The long-board thing narrowed down the possibilities of which surfer he was since the majority of them were using short boards. But there were still at least a dozen long-board surfers on the waves. At the end of the day, she supposed it didn't matter which surfer he was. It wasn't like she could march out into the ocean and demand that he come in to shore and explain himself.

Actually, she didn't give a darn what he had to say for himself. She did have a few things to say to him, however. She'd had the entire drive down from San Francisco to plan her scathing speech, in fact.

Realizing the beachcomber was still standing there, she asked him, "Any idea when the surfers will call it a day?"

"Not till sunset. That's in about an hour-and-a-half."

Impatient to give Trent a piece of her mind, she had no intention of leaving and letting him slip away from her unscathed. She would wait. But it was cold out here. She slogged back to her car to dump her shoes in the trunk and fetch her emergency blanket. Plopped down on a corner of the blanket on the sand, she wrapped the remainder of the wool-plaid throw around her shoulders.

The surfers were mesmerizing. They flew across the waves like ballet dancers with wings beneath their feet. And they looked as fragile as brightly colored butterflies against the towering walls of water crashing down around them. Although the occasional surfer was overtaken by a break and swallowed up for a heart-stopping minute in the frothing surf, most of these guys were really, really good. They safely dropped off the back side of the crests or rode the waves in until they petered out. Then they'd paddle over to the nearest Jet Ski, ride back out and do it all again.

Which one was Trent? She narrowed it down to three or four of the tallest, most powerful surfers. But beyond that, she couldn't tell. The sun expanded into a giant, pulsing ball of red as it slipped below the cloud deck to briefly show itself and then slide behind the sea.

No big surprise, teen girls started filtering onto the beach as sunset approached. Chloe was a bit shocked by the sheer number of groupies and the scantiness of their bikinis in this chilly weather.

The temperature dropped precipitously with the sun, and the last of the surfers grabbed quick waves and rode them all the way in to shore. She thought several of them actually eyed her appreciatively as she searched for Trent. But in light of the nubile, half-naked phalanx of hot chicks swarming the surfers, she probably was mistaken. At thirty years old, she was a senior citizen on this beach.

Trent was one of the last to jog ashore, a bright yellow-and-orange surfboard tucked under his arm. Her heart raced at the sight of him. Or maybe it was anticipation of the confrontation to come making it pound like that. Either way, she hurried to where he bent over his board, unhooking it from its ankle tether.

He glanced up as she drew near. The lanyard slipped out of his hand and fell to the sand as he straightened abruptly.

"What the hell are you doing here?" he demanded, his voice rough like he'd been shouting over the surf and swallowing saltwater all day.

"You and I need to talk," she shouted back over the crashing-ocean noise.

"I've got nothing to say," he growled. "You're convinced that I'm incapable of real feelings or sustaining a relationship. That basically says it all."

Dammit, he'd stolen her line! "And it's over?" she demanded. "Just like that?"

"Yup. Just like that." He picked up his board and commenced hiking up the beach toward a crowded surf shack. Warm, yellow light poured out onto the sand as twilight fell quickly.

She followed him, not about to let him get away with an exit line like that. Although she wasn't at all sure what there was left to say between them. If he could walk away from her without a backward glance like this, then she'd been right about him, after all. He wasn't capable of real feelings or any remotely resembling commitment.

"I loved you, dammit!" she shouted over the roar of the ocean.

Trent stopped a dozen yards short of the surf shack and its raucous crowd of surfers stripping out of wet suits and hoisting cans of beer, staring like she'd just spoken to him in Martian. "You love—" He broke off, looking past her first, and then all around the beach. "Where are your bodyguards?" he demanded.

"I told Jeff I don't need any."

"And he went along with that?" Trent exclaimed. He shoved a distracted hand through his wet hair, standing it up in every direction. "We've got to get you off this beach and under cover!"

"I'm fine. I figured out who was stealing the money from Paradeo. It was Barry. The FBI will find his accomplice or accomplices and the drug cartel will get off my back."

"And until the FBI finds these alleged accomplices? You're still in danger until then," he snapped.

She shrugged. After the pain of the past day, she didn't especially care about being in danger. It was such a small thing in the face of loving and losing Trent. The prospect of decades of gray, lonely years unfolding one after another until she died, bitter and alone, frankly wasn't all that appealing.

"Don't give me that I-don't-care-about-danger look," he growled. Dropping his board, he stepped forward aggressively, took her upper arm in his big hand and steered her bodily toward the parking lot.

"Stop! You're hurting me!"

"I am not, and you know it. Be quiet and let me get you out of here. And then you're telling me what you just said again."

She planted both heels in the sand and managed to bring him to a halt after he dragged her a half-dozen feet. "You can drop the fake-concern act, Trent. I don't buy it anymore. Jeff told me he ordered you to keep an eye on me in Denver as a favor to Sunny. You took that order a wee bit literally, didn't you? I highly doubt he meant for you to sleep with me."

"He didn't order me to watch you until after—" He broke off. "Not now. Get your cute little tush in gear before I toss you over my shoulder and carry you off this damned beach."

He sounded genuinely furious. Reluctantly, she had to admit he probably had reason to be mad at her. Still, his high-handed attitude irritated the daylights out of her. She stomped along beside him rather than give him the satisfaction of bodily hauling her out of here. As they reached the asphalt parking area, a streetlamp flickered to life with a loud buzz, and Trent started violently. Wow. He really was tense. Although, she failed to see why. The threat to her was all but over.

He stopped in front of a sporty SUV. "Get in the car."

"I've got my own car, thank you very much," she retorted.

"I don't care. Get in."

"No! You can't just order me around, Trent. I'm not one of your floozy fan girls."

"Clearly not," he retorted dryly. "I will pick you up and toss you in my car if you continue to be obstinate."

That was it. She'd had it with him. She turned on her bare heel, grinding sand into it painfully, and marched to her car. She grabbed her door handle and Trent's hand closed over hers. It was cold—probably from the ocean, but it still sent heat whipping through her.

"I'll drive," he said quietly.

At least he wasn't yelling at her anymore. She nodded stiffly and slipped her hand out from under his. He took the keys from her and slid behind the wheel as she walked around to the rear and opened the trunk. She slipped on shoes and stowed the blanket and sweater…and never saw the guy coming. One minute she was bent over the trunk, and the next, a large, fast-moving shadow swooped in on her. A powerful arm went around her waist as a hand slapped over her mouth. She was spun and thrown all in one movement. She landed on the floor of a van, slamming to the ribbed metal hard enough to knock the breath out of her.

Tires squealed beneath her and the sliding door slammed shut, enclosing her in darkness. She scrambled upright, hands up in fists.

"Easy, Miss Jordan. I have a gun on you."

Miguel Herrera. Where was Trent? Why hadn't he come roaring to the rescue? "What did you do to my… boyfriend?" She hoped Herrera didn't hear her hesitation.

"One of my boys is keeping him company. He isn't going anywhere until I say so, or until he fancies a gut full of bullet holes."

Oh, God. She was on her own. And as her eyes adjusted

to the van's dim interior, Herrera was, indeed, pointing a gun at her. Along with another man sitting on a crate in the back near the rear doors.

She'd learned very young never to show fear unless she wanted to get eaten alive. The more terrified she was, the more belligerent she knew to act. Right now, she scooted backward until she was leaning against the wall and propped her forearm on an upbent knee as casually as she could muster, even though she felt like throwing up. *Where are you, Trent?* "You keep kidnapping me, Miguel. Why don't you just call me and ask whatever you want to know? It would save us both so much trouble."

"Cool customer," he commented under his breath. Then, louder, "Shut up. When I want you to talk, I'll ask the questions."

Uhh, okay. She was in no hurry to spill her guts to this man. Death was probably in her very near future, but the decision wasn't in her hands at this point. She visually searched the floor of the van for a weapon or something to help her escape, but the vehicle was bare.

Somehow, she didn't believe that Trent would be kept off her trail for very long. For once, she was glad for his freakish speed. He would figure out a way to use it to his advantage and follow her. If nothing else, he would get word to Winston Ops and they would use their scary powers to track this vehicle and send help.

The key now was not to panic and to keep her captors relaxed. Happy even. Hence, she would be as cooperative as she possibly could be until the cavalry arrived. It was a plan, at any rate, and held the encroaching panic at bay.

Chapter 12

Trent saw a flurry of activity in the side mirror, and instinct had him ripping open his door and rolling out of his seat before his brain even registered what was happening. Panic and rage erupted in his skull and his body coiled to spring. Except when his feet landed on the pavement, he registered guns—several of them—trained on him. Even he wasn't proof against that many flying bullets.

He froze, snarling in fury as a man threw Chloe in the back of a van and jumped in after her. The thug in the parking lot in front of him didn't worry Trent. He could take that bastard. But the guy in the passenger window of the van pointing an automatic assault weapon at him with cool precision was another story. Even a bare instant's observation told Trent this guy was a pro who would neither miss nor hesitate to empty a full clip of lead into Trent's gut.

The van peeled out as Trent stared on in impotent fury. The vehicle moved far enough away that the guy in the passenger window no longer had a shot at him, and Trent turned his attention to the single shooter who had been left behind, no doubt to make sure Trent didn't follow the van.

He gauged his chances of reaching the thug's weapon before Herrera's man could pull the trigger. He figured about fifty-fifty. Good enough for him. Chloe was in that van and its taillights were diminishing to specks in the distance. Fast.

Trent leaped, keeping his trajectory extremely low and using every bit of speed his body possessed to close the gap. The guy got off one shot and Trent vaguely registered searing heat in a long line along the back of his right shoulder.

But then he was on the guy, wrenching the pistol out of the man's shocked grasp and putting all his momentum behind the elbow he swung at the guy's face. He was too close to use his fist, but the sharp point of his elbow caught Herrera's man in the right temple and dropped him like a rock.

Trent spun and leaped for Chloe's car. He backed up, running over the downed thug's legs, and effectively ensuring the bastard wouldn't give chase. As the man screamed invectively, Trent stepped on the gas, and Chloe's car peeled out of the parking lot exactly the same way the van had.

Last he'd seen the van, it had been heading west toward the Pacific Coast Highway. As he sped after it, he searched the glove compartment and door pockets for Chloe's cell phone. No sign of it. He had no time to stop and call Winston Ops for backup or he'd lose the van, and Chloe, for good. He was on his own. Swearing, he floored the accelerator and used his reflexes to maximum advantage as he swerved in and out of traffic.

A white van came into sight well ahead of him. *Hang on, Chloe. I'm coming, baby.*

Chloe was tipped over on her side as the van turned abruptly. It felt like they were going uphill. Heading inland, huh? If only she knew this area better she might have some idea where they were taking her. The hard rectangle of her cell phone was comforting in her pants pocket. As soon as the bad guys left her alone, she'd call for help. Funny, but her first thought was to call Trent and not the police. Had she really come to depend on him that much? Did she trust him with her life over anyone else she might call? Like Don and the FBI? Or even the local police?

Shocked, she righted herself and tried to catch a glimpse of something out the windshield that would identify where she was. But sitting low on the floor like this, all she could see was the rapidly darkening sky.

She comforted herself with imagining Trent overpowering the guy Herrera had left behind. Poor schmuck probably hadn't even known what had hit him when Trent jumped him at superhuman speed. She envisioned Trent jumping into her car to give chase and calling in every law enforcement agency on the west coast and Winston Ops to come rescue her—

Wait a minute. What was he going to call with? She had her cell phone with her, and he was wearing a wet suit that didn't have anywhere to store a phone in its form-fitting neoprene. Her heart sank. Trent was on his own, and even he couldn't take out three armed kidnappers all alone, assuming he even made it past the first guy back in the parking lot.

The van drove for maybe an hour. The car noises from outside diminished and the roads got bumpier. They must be taking her someplace nice and isolated to torture her and kill her. Were it not for her complete panic at the notion of never seeing Trent again, never getting a chance to thank him for all he'd done for her, never working up the courage to tell him how she felt about him, she might have dozed off in the darkness and monotony of the ride. But as it was, she started working on the hypothetical speech she was going to give him when he hypothetically overcame the massive odds against him and rescued her from this mess. It was better that screaming in terror.

She was still working on how to properly apologize to him for putting herself in this danger in the first place when the van slowed, stopped, and its ignition turned off.

The guy in the back of the van opened the double doors and jumped out. All she could see were trees behind him.

"Out," Herrera barked at her.

She rose to her feet, bent over, and made her way to the back. Her legs were so wobbly they barely held her weight. They did collapse when she jumped down to the ground. The first thug grabbed her roughly by the arm and yanked her upright. And then, as if thinking better of having helped her, he gave her a hard shove that nearly knocked her over again.

She drew up short when a gun barrel appeared under her nose. "Move," Herrera growled.

Glancing around frantically, she saw they were surrounded by pine trees and a small cabin was in front of her. Wasn't there some kind of national forest not too far from Malibu up in the hills? That must be where they'd taken her. Not that knowing where she was would do her any good if Herrera shot her before she could call Trent.

She stumbled toward the cabin, hoping it had a working restroom. She sneezed when she stepped into the dusty, dark interior. Someone switched on a light behind her and illuminated the filthy room. No one had been in this place for months or maybe years. A thick layer of gray dust covered everything. The furniture was decrepit and broken chairs were stacked in one corner of the main room.

Herrera spoke in rapid Spanish, ordering both his men

to sweep the area outside and then stand guard. Chloe was left alone with him.

"I'm almost afraid to see it, but is there a working restroom in this place?" she asked her captor.

He didn't answer her, but rather moved to a closed door and poked his head inside. He flipped a switch inside the space, and she glimpsed an old-fashioned stand sink below a mirror that had lost much of its chrome finish.

"In there," Herrera grunted. "One minute. After that, I come in and kill you."

Nodding, she closed the door and breathed a huge sigh of relief not to have a gun pointed at her for a few seconds. The toilet was rusty and filthy and the water in it had a green, goopy biology experiment growing in it. Knowing Herrera, he was listening at the door and she was going to have to actually use it. She maneuvered herself in the tight space so she didn't actually have to sit down on the disgusting toilet. She checked the tiny window high on the wall to make sure none of her captors were peering in the window, and she whipped out her cell phone.

She turned the volume all the way down and dialed the Winston Ops number from memory. She stuck the phone in her armpit and pressed down on it frantically lest Herrera hear someone talking from the other end. As it was, she wouldn't be able to speak into the device, but hopefully someone would figure out she was in trouble, triangulate the phone's position, and come to rescue her.

She relieved herself quickly and at least found a few tissues from the moldy box on the back of the toilet. And then she had a sudden inspiration. Herrera was no dummy, and at some point he was likely to search her. Her minute was almost up so, working fast, she burrowed her fingers deep into the tissue box and stashed her cell phone under the pile of tissues.

She flushed the toilet, skipped washing her hands in a sink that was even more disgusting than the toilet and opened the door. Sure enough, Herrera loomed inches from her and she lurched backward, startled.

He grabbed her arm and yanked her out of the bathroom, all but throwing her down onto a wooden chair he'd placed in the middle of the room. As for him, he perched a hip on the corner of the kitchen table.

"All right, Chloe. Enough games. Where's Paradco's money?"

"I don't have it, Miguel." As he took an aggressive step forward, no doubt to backhand her or worse, she added quickly, "But I know who took it."

He subsided back on the edge of the table. "Oh, yeah? I can't wait to hear this."

In line with her scheme of keeping this guy as happy as possible for as long as possible while rescue came, she explained, "Barry Lind was embezzling the money."

Herrera shook his head sharply. "He didn't have access to all the accounts money was going missing from. But you did."

"You're right," she replied. "He either had more than one accomplice inside the company, or he had a top-notch hacker outside the company working with him."

Herrera looked surprised at the admission, but then snapped, "So where's the money now?"

"I have no idea. But if you give me a computer and a few days, I can probably track where it went." That, of course, was a lie. She had no way of getting banks to surrender transaction records to her, and goodness knew, she wasn't a good enough hacker to break into any bank's computer system and steal the records. It would take the FBI's clout to do what she had promised.

Herrera snorted. "You may have been clever enough to steal some money, but you're not that good."

Dang. He'd seen through the lie.

He took an aggressive step forward. "You seem to have no idea exactly who you're dealing with, Chloe. But you've made a terrible mistake stealing from my employer. They kill without a second thought."

"I know exactly who they are, thank you very much," she snapped. "Well, I don't know exactly which cartel it is, but I know I've been laundering drug money for the past six months." As soon as the words were out of her mouth, she knew them for the monumental mistake they were. This was not a man to be that honest with. Particularly not with that pistol in the holster under his left arm.

Herrera reeled back at that. "You knew? And you didn't turn them in?" he demanded incredulously.

Must backtrack hard and fast if she didn't want to get shot in the next sixty seconds. She shrugged. "I think it's insane that drugs aren't legal. At least some drugs. It's not my job to wonder where Paradeo's money comes from. I'm just a bean counter collecting a paycheck and trying to get by." God, she hoped he bought it. She delivered the explanation with as much sincerity as she could pack into her voice.

One of the thugs opened the door and told Herrera in Spanish that the area was clear. Miguel snapped back that they should split up and guard each side of the house. From outside. The thug nodded and left.

"How did you discover that Mr. Lind was stealing money?" Miguel asked, his voice dangerously quiet.

She briefly considered how to answer him. Sticking to the truth as much as possible was her best bet.

"Answer me!" Herrera barked so sharply she about fell off the chair. Lord, that man scared her. The violent look in his eye promised worlds of pain beyond anything she'd ever imagined.

She stammered, "Barry called me when I got back into town after my sister's wedding. He wanted to talk with me." She described in detail her meeting and conversation with Barry, including every detail she could recall. Now it was all about stalling until help came. But finally, she was down to the meat of the matter. She took a deep breath and admitted, "And then he gave me a flash drive. He told me he'd copied every financial record he could lay his hands on, and he wanted me to take a look at them and see what I could find."

Herrera stared. "How did he get every record the company has? He didn't have that kind of access across the board."

She nodded. "You're smarter than I am. It took me until yesterday to ask myself that very same question."

"And?" Herrera sounded genuinely interested.

"Like I said, the only way for Barry to have obtained the records he did was to have help. I have to say I don't think Barry was good enough with computers to have broken into the various compartments of the company's records by himself."

"Neither do I," Miguel answered thoughtfully.

How did he know Barry well enough to have an opinion about the guy? Lind had been murdered within a few days of Herrera arriving at the company. Weird.

"It's not nice to throw a dead man under the bus," he commented lightly.

"Excuse me?"

"Obviously, you were one of Mr. Lind's accomplices. And now that the guy's dead, you're trying to throw all the blame onto him."

"I am not! I was *not* one of his accomplices!"

Herrera's arms were crossed in a posture of patent disbelief, but all he said was, "Convince me."

How on earth was she supposed to do that? She opened her mouth to ask for a computer so she could show him the trail of transactions Barry had used, and how she'd figured out the accounting entries led back to an ISP address that turned out to belong to one Barry Lind. But before sound could come out of her throat, the door burst open.

It was the van driver. He announced in rapid Spanish that a pickup truck had been spotted on the main road headed this way with its headlights off.

Herrera surged up off the edge of the table and strode over to her, grabbing a handful of her hair and yanking her head back painfully. "Who knows where you are?" he demanded harshly.

Her scalp felt like it was about to detach from her skull and tears ran down her cheeks from the sharpness of the pain. "Nobody!" she cried out.

He flung her head forward in disgust, snapping her neck hard enough that it ached. Miguel moved over to the driver. She had to strain to hear him tell the guy in Spanish to guard the driveway and scare off any trespassers.

A pickup truck? Trent would be either be in her car or the small SUV he'd been driving. Had Winston Ops already sent someone out to investigate her open cell phone line? It had only been a few minutes. No way could they have responded already. Who was it, then? She desperately hoped it wasn't some innocent bystander about to be in the wrong place at the wrong time.

The driver left and Herrera turned to her. He looked violent. Angry. But in a few seconds, it was almost as if he…deflated. It was the strangest thing. He pulled the only other chair from the kitchen table over and sat down in it directly in front of her, knee to knee.

"Tell me exactly how you figured out Barry Lind was the thief," he ordered quietly.

His demeanor was so strikingly different from a few moments before she had no idea what to make of it. If he was playing some sort of interrogation head game with her, it was working.

In all the detail she could muster, she described her search of Paradeo's financial records, of spotting the first discrepancies, of tracking the pattern that emerged. "It looked for all the world like I took the money," she confessed. "It was almost like I was being framed."

"By Barry?" Miguel scoffed. "He wasn't that smart."

"Maybe his accomplice is the brains behind the scheme," she replied.

Herrera stared at her hard for a long time, like he was thinking hard. Abruptly he asked, "Who hired you to work at Paradeo?"

Her gaze slid away from his before she realized what she'd done, and she looked back at him hastily. She named the woman in the HR department who had interviewed her, adding, "I don't know who made the final decision. But she must have been the one to recommend me."

Herrera leaned in aggressively. "You're lying. Don't do it again, or you'll regret it. If you want to live past tonight, you'll tell me the whole truth and nothing but the truth."

An ironic choice of words, this hardened criminal quoting the U.S. Court system's oath for witnesses.

"I'll ask you one more time," he snarled. "Who hired you?"

She'd never been any good at lying, and there was no reason to believe she'd get away with it now. But admitting to be an FBI plant was as good as signing her own death warrant. "An interested party asked me to try and get hired at Paradeo and take a look at its books."

"Who?"

"I can't tell you."

"Why not?"

She took a deep breath and told the God's honest truth. "Because you'll kill me if I do."

His brow lowered thunderously and he leaned back hard, staring at her. "Which is it, Chloe? The Feds or a rival of my employer's?"

Wow. He'd drawn the logical conclusion darned fast. It was easy to forget how smart this man was beneath all that brawn and threatening swagger.

Time for one last bit of honesty. "So here's the thing, Miguel. If I tell you, you'll kill me. At this point, I'm better off refusing to talk and enduring whatever torture you have planned for me than I am answering any more of your questions. I think it's safe to say we're done talking."

For an instant, she thought she saw admiration flash in his black gaze. But then he stood abruptly, dumping his chair over behind him with a crash. "So be it," he growled.

Trent was grateful for the pickup truck that had swung in between him and the van. It provided great cover for his smaller vehicle from the van's driver. But as the miles passed and the roads became more and more deserted, worry began to set in. How was it this truck was going in the exact same direction and making all the exact same turns as the van? Was its driver an accomplice of the kidnappers? His suspicion became certainty that the truck was following the van as the miles rolled by. He was looking at four or more kidnappers—no doubt all armed and dangerous—that he was up against. Alone. This night just continued to get worse.

Caution dictated that he drop much farther back than he'd like to, trailing both truck and van from far enough behind that they couldn't make him as a tail. It was dicey, keeping visual contact and not losing the two vehicles. They wound higher and higher into the hills and the road deteriorated to a rutted and poorly maintained dirt road.

The van's brake lights went on and he made out the white blob ahead turning left. The truck continued on. He swore. Where was it going? Why had the kidnappers split their forces? Was the truck heading around back to set a trap for anyone who might try to rescue Chloe?

It wasn't like he had any choice. He'd walk right into their trap if he had to. He'd die before he allowed harm to come to her. The mental declaration shocked him to his core. Not because he wasn't prepared to do his duty and lay down his life—he surely was. He knew he loved her, but was stunned to realize he was willing to die for her.

In spite of her unwillingness to open up or maybe because of it, he loved her. In spite of her prickly exterior, he couldn't get enough of the woman beneath. In spite of her cussed independence, in spite of her lousy self-esteem, in spite of her difficult past.

No, he corrected himself. It was because of all of that that he loved her. She'd survived everything life had thrown at her. She'd raised her sister, kept her little family together as a child herself, managed to scrape together a decent education and to make something of herself. He loved her protectiveness, her fierce loyalty, her determination and drive. She was a hell of a woman. And all those qualities would stand her in good stead now. She just had to hang on a little while longer.

He turned where the van had, squinting ahead into the darkness. He'd turned off his headlights miles ago, and in spite of his eyes being fully adjusted to the night, he could barely see a thing ahead. His progress up the twin tracks of what looked like an overgrown driveway was maddeningly slow.

He paused yet again, window down to listen for the van ahead. This time he heard nothing. Immediately, he eased the car off the track and into the brush. Picking up the pistol he'd lifted off the guy in the parking lot, he slipped out of the car and into the woods.

It didn't take long for him to see a clearing ahead nor to spot an armed man slouching at the end of the driveway. Trent hunkered down to watch for a few minutes and get the lay of the land, even though a terrible need to hurry pressed in upon him. God only knew what was happening to Chloe inside that cabin.

Based on where this guy was deployed, he guessed there was another man on the other side of the cabin as well. He moved off to his right to check it out. Just as he moved out of sight of the first guard, he spotted a second man. But this one was moving stealthily through the trees.

He crept after the guy, his entire body screaming for action. This sneaking around stuff was the complete opposite of how he was designed to function and it took an extreme act of discipline not to explode into motion. It was for Chloe, he reminded himself. His nerves calmed slightly.

The man he was following made his way carefully toward…a third man! This one was armed and leaning against a tree just beyond the clearing that contained the cabin. Trent frowned. What was the sneaking man he was following doing? Playing a practical joke on his buddy? Or had the pickup truck's driver not been an accomplice in the kidnapping after all?

Confused, he followed along. The sneaking man eased a knife out of an ankle sheath and closed in on the third man. There was a flurry of movement. The sneaking man jumped, slashed the guy leaning against the tree across the throat with the knife, and blood erupted everywhere. The guy with the slit throat didn't go down quietly, however. He let out a hoarse cry and grappled with his attacker.

Who in the hell was the guy with the knife?

The first guard came sprinting around the corner of the cabin, and the guy with the knife was about to be outnumbered. The guard with the slit throat wasn't bleeding out fast enough to die before guard number one joined him.

Trent made a fast decision. He didn't know who knife guy was, but he'd taken out one of Chloe's kidnappers, and the enemy of Trent's enemy had just been promoted to the status of friend. He scooped up a fist-sized rock and glided forward, his muscles weeping with relief at finally getting to move quickly. The first guard, focused entirely on the fight in front of him didn't even look to his right as Trent swung in behind him.

It was child's play to race the last half-dozen strides forward and clack the first guard across the back of the head with the rock as hard as he could. The first guard tumbled to the ground, rolled over once, and sprawled unconscious.

The kidnapper with the slit throat was finally collapsing in knife guy's arms, and their struggle was moments from over. Knife guy's back was turned, and Trent took advantage of his unknown friend's distraction to slip back into the woods and out of sight. No sense revealing himself if he didn't have to. For all knife guy would know, the unconscious kidnapper could have tripped on a tree root and knocked himself out.

Trent winced as knife guy knelt down to check the guy he'd hit with the rock and efficiently slit the man's throat. What the hell? The kidnapper was unconscious and out of the fight. There was no need to kill him. Who *was* this violent enemy of the kidnappers? Glad he hadn't identified himself to the man, Trent crouched, still and silent and waited to see what the bastard would do next.

Apparently convinced no more guards lurked out here, knife guy strode across the clearing to the cabin's front porch. Wincing, Trent left the cover of the trees, and the moment the man slipped inside the cabin, he raced at full speed across the clearing to the porch. Heart pounding, he plastered himself beside a window and eased the safety off his stolen pistol.

Miguel advanced menacingly toward Chloe, and for all the world, death glittered in his gaze. So terrified she could only sit there and stare she watched him stalk her. If only Trent were here. What would he do? He'd move really fast—he'd *move*. In a flash of clarity, she realized she wasn't tied down to this chair. She leaped to her feet and picked the chair up, brandishing it like a lion trainer in a cage with a raging lion.

The front door slammed open, and Herrera whirled to face this new threat. A man in dark clothes with mud smeared all over his face leaped through the door and came to a halt, a gun at the ready in his right hand. "Perfect," he purred.

"Thank God. Don!" she cried as he locked the door behind himself.

"You know this guy?" Herrera asked over his shoulder without ever taking his eyes off Don Fratello.

She almost blurted that he was an FBI agent and her boss, but remembered at the last second that Herrera would kill Don if he knew it. "Yes. He's a friend."

"Damn good friend to come in here guns blazing to rescue you," Herrera grunted.

"You've got it all wrong," Don chortled. "I'm not here to rescue Chloe. I'm here to kill her."

Chloe stared, shocked to the core of her being. "What?" she gasped.

Herrera seemed likewise stunned. "What have you got against her?"

"Stupid bitch almost outed me. Thankfully, she left her little message explaining how she'd figured out old Barry's scheme on my personal voice mail and not my work number. As soon as I shut her up, I can put some other dimwit accountant fresh out of school in her place and keep my little operation running."

Revelations were exploding one after another in her head like fireworks on Fourth of July. Don was Barry's accomplice in robbing Paradeo. Of course. With his FBI resources, he'd been able to crack Paradeo's various security codes and pass them to Barry. Poor Barry must've figured out that Don considered him expendable, or maybe Barry just got scared and wanted out of the scheme.

"You killed Barry, didn't you?" she demanded.

"Piss ant chickened out on me. He figured out who really owns Paradeo and freaked out. Got all holier than thou about stopping the damned drug cartels."

More revelations exploded in her brain. Don had hired her because he thought she was so inexperienced that she would never figure out what he was doing. He'd used her as a cover in case he got found out by the FBI. And that meant he'd probably—

"You framed me!" she exclaimed.

His scornful gaze slid off Herrera for an instant to mock her. "Of course I did. No way am I going down for this. Not after I finally got the nice little nest egg I deserve for all my years of hard work."

"Nest egg? You and Barry stole almost twenty million dollars!" she blurted.

Herrera lurched and Don's weapon jerked. "Easy there,

buddy. I'd hate to have to shoot you before I'm done with you."

"What do you want from me?" Herrera snarled. "My bosses are going to chew you up and spit you out when they find out you stole that kind of money from them. You better offer me a hell of a deal to keep my mouth shut."

"I'll do you one better than that," Don replied. "You kill the girl. And then I'll kill you. I'm a hero with the FBI for killing a high-level drug cartel hit man. I'm a hero with the drug cartel for killing the bitch who was stealing from them. Nobody wants me dead, I walk away with my millions and I live out my life sipping Mai Tais on a tropical beach while some hot babe sucks my—"

Herrera reached for his gun and dived for the cover of the table simultaneously, but Don was too fast and too well trained. Two gunshots rang out in quick succession deafening Chloe. Herrera rolled onto his back, arms splayed, still and silent, while a pool of blood slowly formed beneath him. Chloe stared at the downed man in sheer, frozen terror.

Don's pistol swung at her. She braced herself for the impact. "Don't worry, Chloe. You've got a few more seconds to say your prayers. Gotta get Miguel's gun first. Wouldn't do to have rounds from my weapon found buried in your gut. The Mexican shot you, after all. I was tragically a few seconds too late to stop him. But, hey, I gunned him down for you."

Don moved past her to where Herrera lay, and she pivoted to face them, holding the chair in front of her like a shield. Realizing he was no longer between her and the door, she took a step backward. Another.

"One more step and I shoot you where you stand," Don snarled. "And I won't kill you with the shot. I'll let you suffer for a while first. Stray bullet accidentally hit you in the cross fire, you know."

He had all the answers, didn't he? He was supposed to be one of the good guys! Rage and horror roiled in her gut as Don placed Miguel's pistol in the downed man's fingers, wrapping them around the butt and slipping a flaccid index finger into the trigger guard. The weapon lifted toward her.

The window behind her exploded in a fury of flying glass and wood splinters. A large, familiar body arced through the gap, hit the floor, rolled, and came upright between her and Don.

Trent heaved something hard and fast, baseball-pitcher-fashion, at Don. A handful of dirt smashed into the FBI agent's face and he screamed in pain and fury, dropping Miguel's hand to claw at his sandblasted eyes. Miguel's pistol fired, and Chloe instinctively ducked, although the shot had already sailed over her head and into the ceiling.

Trent's gun was against the FBI man's head in a flash. "You so much as twitch, and I'll kill you," Trent snarled.

Chloe took a sobbing breath, her first since Trent had burst through the window, it had all happened so fast. But Don Fratello wasn't an FBI field agent for nothing. He surged up and into Trent, his hands wrapped around the butt of Trent's pistol. The two men grappled, and it looked like about an even fight.

She dived in with the chair, swinging it at Don's back so hard she broke off both back legs. He grunted and heaved, arching Trent backward until she feared Trent was going to break in half. *Ohgodohgod.* Don was winning. She had to do something, but what? Don's hand reached down toward his ankle. He had a hidden weapon there. He was going to kill Trent!

She wasn't close enough to stop the FBI man. She

opened her mouth to scream a warning, but a hand lifted off the floor, yanked the knife out of Don's ankle sheath, and buried it in the FBI agent's calf. Don crashed to the floor screaming profanities. Trent slammed his fist in Don's temple, and the crooked FBI agent went still.

Miguel groaned and dropped the knife with a clatter. Trent darted over to the sofa, tore off a couple strips of the upholstery and brought them back to tie up Don.

Chloe ran forward to kick the knife out of reach and dropped to her knees beside Miguel. She put her hand on his chest to check for a heartbeat and was startled to feel something heavy and padded covering his chest. The gunshot wound in his shoulder was bleeding profusely, and she pressed the heel of her palm against it. Herrera groaned faintly. She stared down at him, grateful he'd helped Trent but mightily confused as to what had just happened.

And then Trent's hands pushed hers aside, and he peeled back Herrera's shredded shirt to look at the bullet wound. "Nasty, but he'll live. Good thing he had on a vest to catch that other bullet. Saved his hide."

Don shifted slightly behind them and Trent moved fast to the FBI man's side and slugged him, hard, in the jaw. The FBI man went limp once more. Trent moved back to her and drew her to her feet.

"Are you all right, baby? Are you hurt?"

"Miguel never laid a hand on me. Are you okay? Don didn't hurt you, did he?"

Trent chuckled. "Never laid a finger on me. I'm too fast for that. Have you got your phone on you? We could use a little backup, here."

"It's hidden in the bathroom." She fished it out of the tissue box and passed it to Trent. He made two phone calls, one to the local police and another to Winston Ops. In under ten minutes, the property was swarming with flashing lights, police, park rangers and even firefighters. Their paramedics declared the two guards whose throats Don had slit dead. Don himself regained consciousness and was securely strapped down to an ambulance gurney while a medic stitched up the gash in his lower leg. He was refusing to say anything to anybody.

It was chaos, and Trent had disappeared somewhere in the fracas to brief someone. He'd promised to return soon, but she didn't see how he'd be back for hours. Chloe sat on the porch steps with a blanket around her shoulders. She wasn't cold, but she desperately needed a hug—a hug from Trent to be more precise—and the blanket was better than nothing.

And once again, she'd managed to end up alone. She must have some sort of special talent for this, and, she had to say, it sucked. She couldn't believe Don Fratello had used her like that. She'd trusted him and he'd set her up. He'd put her square in the sights of a dangerous drug cartel and had planned to kill her all along. What a bastard. Thank God Trent had come along when he had or Don's plan would have worked.

She dropped her forehead onto her knees. Why did men treat her like this? What was it about her that shouted, take advantage of me?

At least the whole mess was over—

Oh, God. *It was over.* There was nothing to hold Trent to her anymore. It truly was over. When he left, he would take her heart with him, and she was pretty sure she would never get it back. Tears came then. And racking sobs that shook her whole body. Cops stomped up and down the steps past her, and none of them gave a darn that her life had just ended.

But then hands stroked her hair gently, and drew her

off the steps and to her feet, into a warm, strong, familiar embrace. "Aww, baby, what is it?"

"You're going to leave me now…and my heart's breaking…and I'm always going to be alone…" Her words were punctuated by great, heaving sobs.

A gentle kiss landed in her hair. "Hold that thought for a minute. There's someone who wants to talk to you, but he has to leave soon. Come with me."

Frowning, she let him lead her across the crowded clearing to the back of an ambulance.

Trent said, "Sweetie, I'd like you to meet undercover DEA agent Miguel Herrera. That's not his real name, of course, but it's good enough for now."

Chloe stared down at Paradeo's security chief, a man who had scared her silly from the first moment she met him. "DEA?" she repeated in shock.

Miguel grinned up at her from the gurney. "Hell of a time I had keeping you alive and unharmed, while convincing the cartel men that I was still a badass. Sorry I had to scare you like that. Couldn't blow my cover."

Snippets of her encounters with him flashed through her head. He never had really hurt her the first time he'd kidnapped her, other than ripping off a few pieces of duct tape. Those momentary flashes of admiration in his eyes. And he'd fallen and knocked out the other thugs chasing her and Trent when they'd fled the Paradeo offices. And tonight. He'd actually been pretty calm with her. He'd let her use the toilet and never searched her. He must have known she'd have a phone and use it somehow to call in help. And most importantly, he'd helped Trent against Don.

She clasped Miguel's icy cold hand gratefully in both of hers. "Thank you," she choked out. "I owe you my life. I'll never forget that you saved Trent's, as well."

He grinned and mumbled, "You're welcome, ma'am. All in a day's work."

Trent told Herrera to take care of himself, and then a pair of medics pushed the DEA agent into the ambulance.

As its flashing lights retreated down the driveway, Chloe murmured to Trent, "He scared me worse than anyone I've ever met, except you."

"I scared you?" he asked in quiet dismay.

She looked down at her feet, embarrassed. A finger hooked under her chin, forcing her reluctant gaze up to his silver one. "Why?"

"You completely messed up my world. I had everything worked out and you came along and screwed up every plan I had, every notion of how my life was going to be." She shook her head and confessed sadly, "I'm never going to be the same. My life is ruined." She looked up hastily. "It's not your fault. I let it happen. I don't blame you."

"Actually, it is my fault."

Her jaw dropped open. "How's that?"

"I knew from the moment you told me there were some things you wanted to try that you were the one woman for me. I did everything in my power to rock your world and blow apart all your silly ideas about order and control and never letting yourself get hurt."

She stared up at him, not sure whether to be annoyed or intensely grateful. She chose to concentrate on the first part. "The one woman for you?" she repeated in disbelief.

Trent spoke in a rush. "Look. I know we haven't known each other that long. And I'm not even remotely close to the normal, boring, safe guy you've always pictured yourself with. But is there a chance you might consider seeing if we could make a go of it?"

Her heart leaped and jumped in her chest like an excited puppy, but she still asked cautiously, "What do you have in mind?"

"I'm thinking marriage and kids and old age and a bunch of grandkids."

Was it true that all her need for structure and order and normalcy had been wiped away by this man? She could hardly believe it herself, but she said, "That all sounds so…normal." She wrinkled her nose at him.

"Well then, how about we travel the world, I teach you how to surf and we have wild, unplanned adventures in between plenty of smoking-hot sex?"

"That's more like it, Mr. Hollings."

"Then we have a deal, Miss Jordan?"

"Really? You and me?" she said in a small voice. Was it possible that all her dreams hadn't been even a pale shadow of the reality that awaited her?

"You and me, baby. Together forever." He kissed his way to her earlobe, and in between nibbles on it, he whispered, "As soon I get you in bed, I'm going to tie you up and make love to you until you agree to marry me."

Her heart full to bursting with joy, she replied, laughing, "Where's my car? Suddenly, I'm terribly, terribly tired and need to lie down in the worst way."

Yup, this man was a whole lot more than a dream. He was the real deal. "I love you, Trent."

"I love you more, Chloe."

Hah. That remained to be seen. She still had a few more things on that list of hers to get through….

* * * * *

*Don't miss the next story in Cindy Dee's
Code X miniseries: DEADLY SIGHT
available January 2013.*

REQUEST YOUR FREE BOOKS!
2 FREE NOVELS PLUS 2 FREE GIFTS!

ROMANTIC
SUSPENSE

Sparked by Danger, Fueled by Passion.

YES! Please send me 2 FREE Harlequin® Romantic Suspense novels and my 2 FREE gifts (gifts are worth about $10). After receiving them, if I don't wish to receive any more books, I can return the shipping statement marked "cancel." If I don't cancel, I will receive 4 brand-new novels every month and be billed just $4.49 per book in the U.S. or $5.24 per book in Canada. That's a saving of at least 14% off the cover price! It's quite a bargain! Shipping and handling is just 50¢ per book in the U.S. and 75¢ per book in Canada.* I understand that accepting the 2 free books and gifts places me under no obligation to buy anything. I can always return a shipment and cancel at any time. Even if I never buy another book, the two free books and gifts are mine to keep forever.

240/340 HDN FEFR

Name	(PLEASE PRINT)
Address	Apt. #
City	State/Prov.	Zip/Postal Code

Signature (if under 18, a parent or guardian must sign)

Mail to the Reader Service:
IN U.S.A.: P.O. Box 1867, Buffalo, NY 14240-1867
IN CANADA: P.O. Box 609, Fort Erie, Ontario L2A 5X3

Not valid for current subscribers to Harlequin Romantic Suspense books.

Want to try two free books from another line?
Call 1-800-873-8635 or visit www.ReaderService.com.

* Terms and prices subject to change without notice. Prices do not include applicable taxes. Sales tax applicable in N.Y. Canadian residents will be charged applicable taxes. Offer not valid in Quebec. This offer is limited to one order per household. All orders subject to credit approval. Credit or debit balances in a customer's account(s) may be offset by any other outstanding balance owed by or to the customer. Please allow 4 to 6 weeks for delivery. Offer available while quantities last.

Your Privacy—The Reader Service is committed to protecting your privacy. Our Privacy Policy is available online at www.ReaderService.com or upon request from the Reader Service.

We make a portion of our mailing list available to reputable third parties that offer products we believe may interest you. If you prefer that we not exchange your name with third parties, or if you wish to clarify or modify your communication preferences, please visit us at www.ReaderService.com/consumerchoice or write to us at Reader Service Preference Service, P.O. Box 9062, Buffalo, NY 14269. Include your complete name and address.

HRS11B

*Something's going on in Conard County's high school…
and Cassie Greaves has just landed in the middle of it.*

Take a sneak peek at RANCHER'S DEADLY RISK
by New York Times *bestselling author Rachel Lee, coming
in November 2012 from Harlequin® Romantic Suspense.*

"**T**here comes a point, Cassie, when you've got to realize that stuff you got away with as a child is no longer acceptable or even legal."

Linc paused, realizing he must seem to be going around in circles. Well, he probably was, between her damned scent and his own uncertainty about what was happening.

"I'll be honest with you," he said slowly. "I'm wondering what's been bubbling beneath the surface at the school that I'm not aware of. That makes me uneasy. On the one hand, I'm trying to paint it in the best light because I know these kids. Or thought I did. I don't want to think the worst of any of them. On the other hand, I guess I shouldn't make too light of it. There have been three transgressions we know about with you. Four, if we add James. I'm not going to dismiss it, but I'm not going to be Chicken Little yet, either. The mind of a teenage male is impenetrable."

She surprised him by losing her haunted look and actually laughing. "You're right, it is. And girls aren't much better at that age."

Girls weren't much better at any age, he thought a little while later as he drove her home. He'd certainly never figured them out.

"Thanks for a wonderful time," she said as he walked her to her door. "I really enjoyed it."

"So did I," he answered more truthfully than he would have liked. He had to bite his tongue to keep from suggesting they do it again.

She was still smiling as she said good-night and closed the door.

He walked back to his truck, keys jingling in his hand, and thought about it all, from the bullying to the rat to the evening just past. The thoughts were still rumbling around when he got home.

Something wasn't right. Something. He'd grown up here, gone to school here, been away only during his college years, and now had been teaching for a decade.

His nose was telling him something was wrong. Very wrong. The question was what. And who.

Find out more in RANCHER'S DEADLY RISK
by Rachel Lee, available November 2012
from Harlequin® Romantic Suspense.

HARLEQUIN®

American ★ Romance®

Discover the magic of Christmas with two
holiday stories of love and forgiveness in

CHRISTMAS IN TEXAS

Christmas Baby Blessings

by TINA LEONARD

Capri Snow isn't happy when she discovers
that the Bridesmaids Creek Christmastown Santa is her
almost-ex-husband and cop, Seagal West. But when danger
strikes, Seagal steps in to protect his wife, no matter the cost.

&

The Christmas Rescue

by REBECCA WINTERS

When Texas Ranger Flynn Patterson saves Andrea Sinclair
and her infant child from her stalker ex-husband, he finds
himself in more danger than just losing his heart.

Bring the magic of Christmas home
this November 2012.

Available wherever books are sold.

HARLEQUIN® *Blaze*™

red-hot reads

Double your reading pleasure with Harlequin® Blaze™!

2 GREAT NOVELS SAME GREAT PRICE

As a special treat to you, all Harlequin Blaze books in November will include a new story, plus a classic story by the same author including…

Kate Hoffmann

When Ronan Quinn arrives in Sibleyville, Maine, all he's looking for is a decent job. What he finds instead is a centuries-old curse connected to his family and hostility from all the townsfolk. Only sexy oysterwoman Charlotte Sibley is willing to hire Ronan…and she's about to turn his life upside down.

The Mighty Quinns: Ronan

Look for this new installment of The Mighty Quinns, plus *The Mighty Quinns: Marcus,* the first ever Mighty Quinns book in the same volume!

Available this November wherever books are sold!

www.Harlequin.com

HB79723